# HER ASSASSIN

MARGAUX FOX

# 1

---

The brief was simple. I don't like simple. I like creative.

If they had wanted a simple killing, they should have hired Rabinovich. Even as his name flickered through my thoughts, I couldn't help but roll my eyes. It was an insult really, that I, Elena Volkova could be compared to such an unimaginative, ignorant, old-fashioned asshole.

Maybe our kill numbers were pretty equal and perhaps we both had an efficiency level that put us in the same category, but numbers are not everything. If I were to kill everyone in the same boring, predictable way I my numbers would be double his, but the devil is in the details, darling. I don't want to be known as a one-trick killer, I want to have flair, passion, imagination ... I take pride in my work. I am, after all, the best.

I inched along the concrete outdoor window box. It would almost be pleasant were it not for the gale-force wind and being 36 stories high. I could have taken this target out in numerous secluded locations. He had, in fact, just finished a ski holiday in the Alps that would have provided ample opportunity for "an accident"—but where was the challenge in that? This death was to be a statement, not an accident. No point at all in being the best if no one can admire your work.

I flipped the magnet from my back pocket and trailed it down the edge of the window. I felt the tiny pull as it found the catch, and I knelt, flicking the magnet up and down until it caught the latch fully, and with a slow click came undone. At this height, the safety latch would only allow the window to open a couple of inches, but now it would open enough for a lithe assassin like myself to slip inside.

I'm not tiny, but I am lean. I've trained highly in gymnastics and it helps me take on adventurous missions that others won't.

My feet landed on the soft cream carpets, a luxury that was not custom in Italy, but when you were running an international cartel business that was currently booming, you could afford the fancy suites. I flipped through the minifridge; all the bottles were untouched. I helped myself to the vodka. It was expensive and reminded me of home—we all need those home comforts now and again. Like the smell of fresh blood, the taste of vodka, and the Russian cold that makes your bones ache.

I caught my reflection in the full wall mirror. My white-blonde hair was neatly tucked away and replaced with dark curls. I had taken a spray tan too; I liked the bronzed look on occasion, although my pearly paleness suited my natural bright blue eyes better. But today I was blending into the Italian crowd so I had worn hazel contacts. Today I was any other italian woman.

I always enjoy the changing of myself. I

always enjoy that I can become anyone that I need for any job. There are certain advantages to being a woman that male assassins don't have. Not ever being seen as a threat is one of them. Being vastly underestimated is another. Cultural misogyny sometimes has its advantages.

He would enter the lobby in less than five minutes, take the lift up, make his way into the bathroom, and whilst washing between his legs he would send for a local call girl. I've been studying him, I know. People are creatures of habit. People are dangerously predictable. I had considered that option but his tastes were too vanilla to even entertain it, one of the girls I spoke to had even used the phrase *spooning sex*. Surely that's what a wife was for, not the high-end hookers he was splashing the cash for. Well, at least he paid, unlike many assholes I had met.

I made my way into the luxurious bedroom, the bed looked bigger than my own super king and I eyed it up enviously. I went to the wardrobe and fiddled with the back panel until it came open with a pop. Spooning sex wasn't the only thing Loretta had told me about. "Bingo!" I said with a smile as my fingers curled around the pound bag of premium cocaine.

I heard the lift *ping* down the hallway and I edged to the corner and slid behind the back of the bathroom door. Nico was on the phone when he entered, but it was obvious, he was in a hurry to wrap up the conversation. It was done in seconds and he tossed his phone to the side with a frustrated sigh. Like clockwork, he entered the bathroom, and his hands dropped to his belt as he flicked on the tap.

I moved like lightning but with grace; the door sprang closed behind him and before his gaze had even reached mine his head was smashed with a force against the mirror. It wasn't enough to kill him, but enough to daze him. I watched as he slid down the marble counter into a bloodied heap, his hand still on his cock...like that would ever be my aim. I raised my foot and pressed with a force on his shoulder, spinning him to face forwards. Even in his dazed condition, he was starting to get his surroundings, and I watched his fingers curl, preparing to strike.

"Tut-tut, Nico, you should never hit a woman," I murmured with a condescending sigh as I raised my foot, the curve of my heel pressing his head backward with a hard crack against the marble. The second crack was enough to leave him pretty out of it now. One more would do the trick, but instead, I pulled open the corner of his cocaine stash. With one gloved finger I guided his chin backward and pulled his bottom lip down, pouring in copious amounts of narcotics. I watched him inhale, choke, then try to spit out the powder, but we both know it is too late. His gums would be numb already, cocaine hitting his bloodstream in a heated rush. I continued to pour, covering him and filling his mouth as much as I could. There are worse ways to die; I hope at least the drugs will take off the edge. Reaching in my pocket I took out the razorblade, with six deep lines across his inner wrists, my work was done. His death would be slow...ish. His blood will flood the bathroom floor, spilling from the cuts until his heart has nothing left to pump, maybe the last thing he will see are my initials carved into his skin with the question of who... why... how... lingering on his dying lips.

Or maybe the cocaine will have him thinking he is in heaven before his eyes even close. Who knows?

I check myself in the mirror wiping any remnants of blood from my skin. My choice of dress was a simple black shift- it never shows bloodstains and allows me to move easily. I left the way I came, sure to fasten the latch behind me. I like to leave a little mystery after all.

I TOOK a first-class flight to France. It is only a two-hour flight, but the client pays expenses and getting home in luxury is what I consider a necessary expense. The overhead is stuffed full of airport shopping; not a necessary expense but I have a range of aliases I need to keep in style. Not that style matters too much where I am going.

I have my city apartment in the very heart of Paris and I am in love with it. When I want fine dining, boutique shopping, and an official place to call home it ticks all the boxes. In my early twenties, I had fallen in love with the romance of Paris. My addiction to expensive shoes, overpriced purses, and catwalk style had no other true home than the Champs-Elysées. Having money when you are in your twenties creates these addictions. Growing older though, and losing the only person I had ever known love from, I had found my new roots. My true home is miles from the bustling Parisian streets out in the rustic French countryside.

It was the first thing my mother taught me. "Elena, don't ever trust that voice on the end of the line because one day it will be your name they whisper on someone else's list." I mean we don't do the dial-ins anymore like she used to; my kill list comes through a series of encrypted untraceable telegram messages, but still, I took the essence: Find a good place to stay under the radar.

I had stumbled across the crumbling french estate a few years ago. It had cost me a lot more than I would care to admit on getting it back into habitable condition, and even more to add my own "El flair," but

I was happy with it. I get paid a ridiculous amount to do the work I do so money really is no object. Cool crisp winters, budding springs, glorious summers, and colorful falls offered everything, all year round.

It was also home to my bestest friend in the entire world. The one guy I absolutely depend on without a second thought. "Kittttttt!" I cried as the imposing steel gates opened at my retina scan and I bounded down the driveway towards the huge brick chateau. I knew wherever he was he would hear me, and sure enough in just a few moments, I saw his gorgeous thick red and white Japanese Akita fur hurtling towards me. Dropping down onto my knees, I left my bags strewn across the driveway as I bundled him up in my arms for slobbery licks and snuggles.

"Oh, you are such a good boy. Who is mummy's good boy? Give me all those kisses. Mwah." I had rescued Kit a few years ago. Well, I use the term *rescued* loosely. I was on a job when he had hurtled towards me mid-garrotting; it went against all my principles to hurt an animal so the prospect of inflicting any kind of pain on a dog as beautiful as Kit gave me genuine heartache. Luckily for me and Kit, he was much fonder of me than his, at the time, dying owner. His snarly teeth brushed against my throat only for a second before his tongue peppered me with dog kisses. It was a mutual adoration. I hadn't, of course, planned my exit with a 100 lb Akita, however, Kit almost seemed to know that stealth and inconspicuousness were key and happily trotted down the street beside me wearing a makeshift slip leash I had created out of the dead guy's leather belt.

From that moment my inner circle grew from one to two to now three. Kit was my reason to find a home, to have a place to return to, but he had also proved a slight issue when it came to the nature of my job. I couldn't exactly take him with me across the world and that had meant opening the door to...

"Hi, Aveline." I watched her panic subside as she rushed around the corner to find me, making her way over she collected my strewn bags from across the driveway muttering in French under her breath. I tried not to grin. Aveline is a local girl who I found coincidentally but has proven to be the stabilizing factor my home needed. Although she is over ten years younger than me, she certainly acts twice my age. She has that bustling older woman aura that seems to emit calm and stress in equal doses.

Kit at a first glance may seem almost indifferent to Aveline's presence, but I have observed them both when neither knew I was watching and the bond is there. Kit's nonchalance is only a typical akita act; secretly he loves Aveline's homemade cooking, soft strokes, and her inability to keep up with him when they go for a run.

Aveline may grumble at me but there is a loyalty that will never be broken. Whilst she grew up just a few miles away, Aveline will never return to her home village. Her past there haunts her, and though I could not offer her an escape from memories, I have given her a way to leave abuse and stifling control behind. She has no idea what I do for a job, if she were the type to speculate, I would guess she would think something exotic, but she rarely asks questions. That is the beauty of Aveline; in order to be an exceptional service provider one must be able to see what is required or not required and do just that. She studies in her free time—she wants to maybe be a chef one day—and she lives in and takes care of my chateau and of my beautiful Kit.

There will be a time one day that she will leave the safety of my chateau gates behind, but it doesn't seem something that will happen in the immediate future. She is happy and I, in turn, have grown to like her and trust her. I'm not exactly fond of humans in any capacity; I rarely tolerate them, but Aveline has a tenacious will that I find endearing, and Kit is a good judge of character. His approval has gone a long way in securing her place within my heart. That and she makes a mean-ass cupcake.

"If I had known you were due home today, I would have made something special for you," she said with pursed lips.

"Oh, hush your moaning and look in the big brown bag." I watched as her lips threatened to curl into a huge smile as she opened the paper bag that I brought from an Italian deli in Naples. It is filled with random things that I thought she might be able to use in some mouth-watering Italian dish. "Oh, El! I can make us some real pasta! Oh, and what about some cheesy calzones? Tiramisu? Or how about a Tiramisu ice cream, that could be really amazing! Ouf, this is perfect! Merci!"

"Don't thank me, it was purchased for purely selfish reasons," I said with a smile as we made our way inside, and before long wafts of Italian herbs and rich sauces spread through the house making my tummy rumble with a pang.

## 2

*Inventive but what a fucking mess.*
    *Next time think like a Russian...*
*Clean. Efficient. No stains.*
    *The next target will need thorough research.*
    *Maybe even an ACCIDENT!!*
    *Katherine Scott-Webb, ex-wife of next British PM.*
    *C L E A N ! ! ! ACCIDENT!!!*
    *El: DO NOT FUCK UP.*

My tut was audible, if he wanted an accident, I could give him an accident. I can do clean. I am brutally efficient with a sniper rifle. It just may not be one in the conventional sense. I suppose the where, when, and how would all depend on the who.

I was fresh out of my gymnasium, I have a top of the range gym and calisthenics playground in the basement of the chateau-think Ninja Warrior- bars, rings, high platforms all kinds of things for me to play on. I also have a similar one outdoors in the chateau grounds which is where I train on a nice day like today. I like to create courses to challenge myself on and race through them as fast as I can. I like to be prepared for anything. In my line of work, it is the least you can do.

I stripped and showered quickly, as usual excited by the prospect of a new target. There was a rush this job brought with it that was second to none.

I flipped open my encrypted Mac and hit the top-secret search engine of ...Google.

### Katherine Scott-Webb

Half an hour later and Katherine Scott-Webb had not piqued my interest further than the fact she is a female. I didn't normally find women on my list. It didn't make a huge difference to me in some ways but then in others, it wasn't exactly my favorite. I could usually find a way to justify any of my killings. Most were scum-of-the-earth asshats that didn't deserve even the creative deaths I gave them; in fact, they should be dropped in the middle of the ocean with no further thought given. Women often didn't have the narcissistic qualities of men, generally speaking, and whilst I had no issues killing a female who deserved it, I didn't love the prospect of killing a woman for a man's political gain.

Katherine Scott-Webb was the ex-wife of a prominent British politician who was tipped to be the next British Prime Minister. Now the ex-husband, he did look like an asshat.

Most people did deserve it though, one way or another. I had yet to meet an innocent person who ran in these circles. They all had a game to play. An agenda. A person to fuck over. So, who was Katherine Scott-Webb, and what were her crimes?

I image searched Katherine Scott-

Webb and I was surprised, her Wikipedia page listed her as fifty but she looked a good ten years younger. It seemed that whilst her ex-husband had been busy politically climbing since their divorce years ago, she had strived to build her own worth. Her company now made the Times 100 list in the UK as one of the best marketing firms to work for, and as a boss, she seemed to have nothing but glowing reviews.

She did have an air about her of privilege. She was dripping British Upper Class from every pore. It wasn't exactly her fault, people who were born into money couldn't help that self-entitled strut they had in their walk and poker that had been inserted up their ass from a young age. There was something else too that I couldn't put my finger on. There was this braveness, a power that exuded from her like an inner strength. I leaned back in my swivel chair and took a loud bite of my apple as her voice echoed around the room. She had given a speech that had been put on YouTube just a few months ago. When would people ever learn? In just a few minutes I could tell so many things about Katherine Scott-Webb.

For example, she is left-handed but plays a sport, I would guess tennis, with her right, which gives her a little ambidexterity. Her hair is long and naturally brown but she darkens it just a shade or two more more and she goes like clockwork for her root touch-ups at Salon Roux in Knightsbridge. Her nails are her own, not fake, but she goes to a small salon round the corner from her house and they use gel shade 057 Cherry Blossom every time. Her outfits are expensive, bought at stores that fit them to her so they would fit no one else as they fit her. The tiny nip at her slim waist and flair over her hips is classy but with a hint of a womanly curve that gives a sexy allure. She stands with her weight favoring her right side and when she says something controversial her hand brushes her ribs as though to shield herself in a defensive pose. She wears contact lenses, I can tell from the shimmer as the studio light catches her irises, but I couldn't see the tell-tale signs of Botox, pinning, or any surgical enhancements—her youthfulness was natural.

Her eyes are green, but not dazzlingly so. The shade of green that is easily mistaken for brown by those who don't look closely. I look closely.

Watching her live, she is strikingly beautiful, not just physically, but in what radiates from her. She seems lovely. But I learnt a long time ago that people aren't always what they seem.

My research job was made easier by the fact she is a more public figure and isn't trying to hide. Between her business, Wikipedia page, and social media account I could locate her office, home, and frequent hangouts. It took me less than five minutes to access her google calendar, which opened up her entire schedule to me as well as her check-ins for the past three years which I would guess to be around the time she didn't opt-out of some tracking app.

All that put together gave me a very deep insight into the life of Katherine Scott-Webb. The only unanswered question would be *why*. What threat did she possibly pose to her ex-husband? What secret was she hiding that he felt must be

protected at all cost? I had a sneaking suspicion it would be something to do with the
un-detailed meeting she had scheduled for
Friday. Which instantly became top of my
to-do list.

"Aveline..." I hollered from my chair. Kit
didn't even shuffle at my feet, but I heard
the clatter of pans from the kitchen, and I
gave a little sigh. *Always on edge, that girl.* "I
have to go to work again. Better freeze some
of whatever you are baking."

LONDON IS AN INTRIGUING CITY. It isn't ro-
manticized like Paris or Rome, I suppose
that is the art of Latin, the ability to weave
stories of budding affection and starry-eyed
lovers that makes even the plainest of
buildings seem charming.

Not that London doesn't have its fair
share of romances associated with it, it just
doesn't have that same feeling. I am a fan of
the clash of old and new. The historical
buildings and Victorian architecture that
seemed to run at odds with glass floor-to-
roof facades and dominating skyscrapers

that line the horizon from all angles. You can stand in Trafalgar Square and be oblivious to the National Gallery that runs its parameter, or meander the Thames and stumble across the ever-spinning London Eye.

The shopping in London is unrivaled, the parks are still green and well kept, the streets are filled with the bustling clash of cultures and diversity. London is a city I can appreciate on so many levels. All, that is, except the weather. I know what you are thinking, I am Russian. We are used to awful weather. That is true, I know how to keep warm when my eyelashes have frozen. But please find me a person who can truly be prepared for the unpredictable weather of Britain.

I had decided to go for *scrupulously clean* rather than *accident*. It was boring, but then, the target seemed too good for anything elaborate and statement like. I thought an anonymous assassination would be ideal. I knelt low against the neighbor's flat roof. The good thing about the fancy neighborhoods is that they even pay people to clean the roof and guttering so the rich people don't look twice about someone who looks like a young man in workman's attire and helmet with a workman's bag on a rooftop. We don't give a fuck about these things in Russia, but I appreciate the courtesy as I set up my scope and laid flat against the asphalt. The wind was negligent, which made a nice change. I adjusted the rifle, the laser lined up to perfect accuracy. I know he suggested an accident, and this was very bland for me, but I don't like being told what to do and I felt like Katherine Scott-Webb deserved a clean death. She had done nothing to warrant a long death, a loss of dignity, or any form of suffering. In fact, I was having a sudden crisis of conscience. Did Katherine Scott-Webb really warrant my bullet at all? My finger stroked the trigger, I watched as she paced back and forth in her bedroom. She was on the phone; from the smile and tilt of her head, it was not work. Not a lover either. Maybe her son. Through my eyepiece, I could see her chest rising with each breath she took. Her last one could be on her lips at any moment with just a light pull—she wouldn't even know. It would all be over in the blink of an eye and the end would come in the time it took for her to fall to the floor.

I couldn't let this be the last word her son heard from his mother. With resolution, I unfolded the stand and carefully dismantled my rifle back into my workman's bag. I looked so much like an eighteen year old boy today in my baggy clothes and I replaced my helmet with a cap. I made my way across the roof, checking the street first, then sliding nimbly down the drain pipe and walking along the street like it was the most natural thing in the world. I needed a new plan.

I SAT on the corner of Grove Street the following day perched on a wall, which looked normal about five minutes ago when the sun was shining and the breeze refreshingly cool. Now, the rain was hammering down so hard I could see the rain bouncing as it hit the puddles. My wig was ruined, my cute ankle boots would never dry the same and my orange blazer was doing very little to keep me dry.

The good thing was that my own hair was safely tucked away, my blonde locks don't love a sudden drenching. I had gone for an auburn wig this time; it had been a while since I had been a redhead and I liked how the honey brown contacts looked with the choppy red bob. I bounced off the wall and splashed in the puddles; I was wet already so why not.

Katherine Scott-Webb lived in a swanky postcode. I knew I would draw attention from the twitchy curtain parade. My presence would never go unnoticed so I had embraced that with my camera, wide-eyed American, Oh-My-God-everything-is-just-so-cool expression and loud phone calls where I was absolutely certain I was on the same street that Hugh Grant lived on.

Whilst my trip hadn't been exactly fruitful, I had been able to take a lot of photos of Katherine Scott-Webb's house. She had standard security; I could disable the alarm in the time it would take to open the front gate. She had a son, but he lived away at university, and I had seen no evidence of a lover in her life. The one thing I had really wanted to scope out was if she had a cleaning person. Everyone else in these kinds of neighborhoods did, but as yet I hadn't found any indication she had one and that was the last thing I needed, an interruption.

*Always take care of the little details. If you are entering a target's home, be sure you know who else has a key.*

I made my way back to my hotel, taking the back entrance so as not to draw attention to the fact my appearance had changed dramatically three times in the past three days. What I needed now was to get closer to Katherine Scott-Webb. I needed to get access to her thoughts.

I checked her calendar and she had a working dinner tonight in the city at 7 pm. I felt the tingle of excitement. I *love* an evening dress-up and role play. I love those moments when I can really stalk my prey in person. The thrill is a buzz like no other. The times when I can taste their cologne, see the curls of their hair, and yet they are oblivious to who I am and to what our next encounter would bring.

I stripped as I walked around my hotel suite, discarding my soaked outfit one layer at a time. My wig went straight in the bin. Standing at the huge bathroom mirror I leaned forward and peeled the brown-tinted lenses from my eyes and watched as my brilliant blue irises came into focus. Stepping back, I gave myself an analytical once over. My body is in perfect peak condition, the height of physical fitness, but needed to look feminine tonight. I pondered outfit choices that would give me that look. I slipped into the shower and flicked the handle, letting the hard jet of hot water pound against my pale skin.

My nipples hardened under the pressure and then softened with the heat, a constant stimulation. That rush of adrenaline made me needy for a release.

I pick up women in lesbian bars or on dating apps when I need release. There were a couple of women I had chatted to on an app since I had been in London, but the idea of them wasn't exciting me. Or I could go into Soho, to a lesbian bar and see who I could meet. The idea didn't thrill me and normally, I *love* Soho. I do a dress up, I do a fake name, I bring them back to my swanky hotel and I have *all* kinds of fun with them.

But something was bugging me. Standing in the shower with my eyes closed against the water all I could see was her. Katherine Scott-Webb. Her breasts as they rose and fell in a blouse and skirt suit that was supposed to be classy rather than sexy, but somehow it was both. The nip of her waist and the way her skirt grazed over the round of her ass.

The way her hands moved as she spoke, elegant fingers, minimal jewellery, neat nails. Her mouth as it moved when she spoke, her make up neutral, the features of her face beautiful, her eyes that were full of depth and soul.

*For fuck's sake, El. She's a target. We don't crush on targets.*

Except I was. I had to admit it to myself, I was crushing on the target.

I reached for the expensive shower cream and covered my fingers and palm in thick, coconut-scented cream. Turning down the pressure I let my hands roam my body.

I know how to take myself there, but I

didn't want to rush. I wanted to enjoy the moment. I let the water continue its constant run against my nipples as my palm slid down over my stomach to rest on the soft rise of my mound. My fingers trailed over myself, slowly, purposefully, building towards something. Katherine was in my thoughts as I touched myself.

My gasp was lost in the rising steam of the shower as my middle finger slid inside my body. I slowly fucked myself, letting my finger curl up and run against my inner walls while my thumb ran against my clit. It felt so good. I imagined her for a second, Katherine, on her knees in the shower with me, her graceful fingers inside me, her lovely mouth on my clit.

My breath quickened, my moans growing louder and louder as my toes curled and my thighs tensed. I felt the build, my orgasm rising with a shuddering heat. I let go and enjoyed the hard spasm of my body against my fingers. I rode each wave as the water ran hot against my flushed skin. I didn't slow until the sensitivity became too much and even then, I thought about pushing through and chasing that next toe-curling, head-spinning high, but I didn't. I let my body recover as I soaped my skin and washed my hair.

I took comfort in the slow, therapeutic movements, letting my fingers trail through the knots in my hair. Working out the kinks as my breathing slowly returned to normal and the shower washed away the sticky trail of my lust down my inner thigh.

Getting off thinking about a target was a new one for me. But, these things happen.

As soon as I came, I felt better for it, satisfied but alert and focused. Ready to hunt my prey.

## 3

I stepped into the fancy Chelsea restaurant as though I belonged, and based on my bank balance, these bitches better fucking believe I did. My black Chanel dress wasn't a custom fit but it looks like it could be the way it rides the curves of my hips and ass. The black sexy lace of the tops of my stockings were just visible each time I took an exaggerated stroll, hips rolling so my ass gave a nice firm bounce.

"What do you mean my reservation is not on the list?" I kept my accent British with that short clip and exaggerating the ending to my question. My voice dropped lower in the way very wealthy people do when they are super annoyed and want to be even more intimidating by saying less. The girl didn't look the slightest bit concerned. In fact, I would consider hiring her for the number of fucks she did not seem to give about her job role, and I honestly couldn't blame her. She must get a ton of women acting like me daily, real pains in the ass with no knowledge of actual real-world problems.

"The reservations are taken weeks in advance and are confirmed by a personalized message and reference number three days before your reservation. Perhaps if you could share with me your booking reference, I will be able to clear the matter up quickly for you." She gave me a sweet smile, which I knew was to mask her smirk. She knew, as well as I did, that I did not have a reservation. However, what I did have was Katherine Scott-Webb's reservation number from her calendar. I pulled out my phone with my own sickly sweet smile.

"Of course, my reservation number is 6-9-4-7-5-1-8-2." I read each number slowly and deliberately waiting until she entered each one in her keypad. She was waiting for it to say that I was mistaken, but there it was, plain as day, my Katherine Scott-Webb's reservation flashed up.

"My apologies, Ma'am. You do have a reservation for today, but your name is not showing on my system. Please take a seat at the bar and someone will be over shortly to lead you to your table." Her voice was monotone throughout her entire speech. I have no idea if she believed me or not but it seemed that if the number shows, I get a table.

I hovered for a few seconds as I felt the cold gust of wind behind me as the restaurant doors swung open once more. I knew she was due, and smelling the scent of Gardenia Les Exclusifs de Chanel—I read in an interview that it was her one splurge she bought herself every Christmas; I actually bought some in Paris before I flew over and, although I enjoyed the scent, in my opinion, it wasn't worth the $3,800 price tag--anyway, I digress. Smelling the scent, I knew it was her approaching. I turned slowly with a low exaggerated spin on my heel. I caught Katherine Scott-Webb's reflection in the tinted glass walls and I knew I would catch her with the swing of my Fendi bag.

As designer extravagances collided, my grip held firm and her strap slipped from her slim shoulders, and her purse landed on the floor.

"Oh, my goodness! I am just so sorry!" I exclaimed as I dropped to the floor in a flustered reach. Katherine Scott-Webb looked startled, caught off guard for a moment, and then she too lowered to her knees.

If photos made her look ten years younger, they really weren't doing the reality justice. Katherine Scott-Webb was stunningly beautiful in a completely natural way. I could see the brush of makeup, the curl of mascara, and the rouge of blush along her cheekbone, but not much more. Her dress was similar to mine in style; I did that on purpose, I admire her taste and I wanted to feel how she would look on me. Classy, sexy, yet elegant at the same time. Katherine was a mistress of never showing too much flesh, but still being so sexy in the way she moved, in the way she is.

Although she was married to a powerful man and had years in the spotlight, and was now head of a multi-national, multi-million-dollar business, she didn't carry herself with confidence I had expected. Instead, she seemed what I call *surface confident-* confident to the eye that doesn't look too closely, but when you scrutinise her, she is uncertain of herself, questioning her every move as our eyes locked for the first time.

I was instantly aware of the fact that she had seen me in my natural state, but that had been my choice. Bright blue eyes and natural blonde hair greeted her inquisitive glance, and for a fleeting second, I had the feeling as though she could see straight past the façade and deep into the real El. But it ended as quickly as it came with the light buzz around my wrist as my watch told me that I had cloned the phone that lay in her purse. Technology really is brilliant these days.

I stood and with a smile I offered her the bag. She rose slowly and I felt her gaze travel over me. It was slow and lingering, assessing as though she had seen me before but couldn't place exactly where. The feeling for me felt alien. I was so used to blending, to never really being seen. Never being noticed until it was too late, the only time my victims would see my face again would be if there was some kind of afterlife.

But Katherine Scott-Webb was different and my intrigue exploded. I didn't even feign heading to the bar. Instead, I left the restaurant with my mind in chaotic over-drive. I needed to know more, I had to have more answers. I found a quieter spot in a cafe that sold overpriced lattes and dried-out cakes. I took out the phone that was now a complete clone of hers and began to search.

The answer it seemed was not hard to find as to why her ex-husband wanted her dead.

What surprised me more is the fact he hadn't had it done sooner.

Katherine Scott-Webb was writing a book.

. . .

*I WAS seventeen when I first met James Webb. I liked him, everyone liked him, he was charming and handsome, and even then it was clear that he was going places. His political ambition was strong even then. Our family, whilst full of titles and a grand yet crumbling house, was not as wealthy as it seemed. So when James Webb asked me out on a date, I felt honoured.*

∽

*IT WAS SOON after we were married that things changed, that I started to see the real James Webb. It was as though in marrying him, I became owned by him, and it wasn't a great place to be.*

∽

*IF I WANTED to go out by myself, if I wanted to wear certain things... suddenly there were all these restrictions on my life that I had to abide by.*

∽

HE WANTED me to be thinner, so I ate less and less until I thought I might fade away completely.

~

IT BECAME HARDER to predict what was allowed and what wasn't. I felt anxious and on edge all of the time.

~

I HAD to wear clothes that hid the bruises that were regularly on my arms. Hiding bruises on my face or neck was harder. Stage make up helps, but I still had to lie and make up stories about how I had hurt myself.

~

HIS RAGES TERRIFIED ME.

~

I WANTED TO LEAVE, so many times, but soon I was pregnant and everything became harder. He said I could never take his son from him. He *had so much power. I knew if I left, I would leave without my child. So, I sacrificed myself for my boy. I wish there had been another way.*

IT SEEMED MORE about her recovery and therapy than trying to sabotage James Webb's political career, however, the implications were there as loud as day. Whether there was any hard evidence wouldn't matter, people would believe this book. Everything about Katherine and the way she wrote was utterly credible. There would be no career for James Webb should the book be released; he would never hit his ambitions as Prime Minister and for me, that was no great shame.

In fact, if anything, taking this guy down should be cause for a celebration. It did cause me a dilemma. Killing women was already not on my list of favorite things to do. Killing women who had suffered years of domestic abuse for standing up and telling their story? Less so.

The book was the story of her life but it also included a tell all on her marriage to

James Webb. As I read further, I felt like I knew Katherine intimately. I felt the pain that she had been through. There was a harrowing chapter involving the miscarriage of her second pregnancy which threw him into a violent rage and he beat her, claiming she lost the baby on purpose.

Katherine Scott-Webb so far had only shown me reasons why she did not belong on my list. Was I missing something? Was there more to her than I was seeing? I needed an in into her life. Observing from a distance was not working for me. Or at least it wasn't working in my employer's favor.

She and I had now met and she was an observant woman. I had no doubt she would recognize me again even in disguise, which meant I needed to think out our next meeting very carefully. Through her book, I had an advantage, a way in because I knew her intimately.

I read each page of her book carefully. I didn't skip a word or skim a line; I took in each carefully curated sentence and I took the journey with her. She did grow up with money in the sense that her father had some ridiculous British title, but in terms of actual wealth, there didn't seem to be so much of it. A lot of her lifestyle was granted to her based on name alone, and with a name, came a responsibility.

She was introduced to James Webb at just seventeen and whilst he was already approaching thirty, he wanted her and who wouldn't? I found old photos of her on google, they spoke for themselves; she was breathtakingly beautiful, a real english rose type with big doe eyes, pale skin and a warm smile that could melt even the thick Russian snow. James Webb was chiseled, handsome, rich, and had that stature of someone who always got what they wanted, an Eton boy through and through. He wanted a young, beautiful meek wife who had a good pedigree, and he found all that and more in Katherine Scott-Webb.

The problem, though, was politics did not always run smoothly. James Webb could not control the arch of his political career as thoroughly as he may have liked, and not long after his perfect wedding to the perfect bride did he find that out. It seemed to the outside world that James

Webb took his professional knockbacks with a calm mind and a cool head, but behind closed doors his need for control manifested in the complete dominance of his wife.

Katherine Scott-Webb's book was not complete and the last few chapters I read painted a vivid picture of mental and physical control by a narcissist.

Closing the screen, I was desperate to know more and also beginning to feel very clear on one thing: If what she was writing was all true, I would not be able to kill Katherine Scott-Webb.

# 4

---

I had debated the best way to verify Katherine Scott-Webb's story. I would need to meet her in person and insert myself in her life, but it was not a guarantee in any case that what she says happened actually did happen.

But no one can ever truly know what occurs behind closed doors unless you are actually behind them. This was why I found myself sitting in first class on a rickety very un-first-class seat on my way up to Manchester. Daniel Scott-Webb was currently studying at the university and from my expert stalking skills I hadn't come up with much. He seemed to be a quiet boy who was reluctant to use any form of social media and made no connection to his father in a public forum, favoring to stay entirely out of the spotlight.

His biggest presence online was under a pseudonym on a Reddit feed that regularly gained traction. It seemed that what Daniel Scott-Webb lacked in public confidence he was not shy to express under the anonymity of a Sub-Reddit Feed. His opinions were diverse but mainly zoned in on British politics. He spoke clearly and with logic and reason. It was obvious he had insight into that world that others did not and this gave him popularity.

He was studying a form of social science... an ism of some kind that he seemed well suited for. Katherine Scott-Webb was certainly proud of his achievements, if their messages were anything to go by, and Daniel Scott-Webb definitely had a high opinion of his mother too.

The texts were only surface deep though. I never found a mention of her book or his father. It was unclear to me as to whether James Webb played a role in his son's life at all. James certainly referenced his son in his political speeches, but then again, I suppose an absent father doesn't do well with opinion polls.

So, I had made the impromptu decision to get access to Daniel Scott-Webb. I wanted to know the truth about his mother and his father and then I would make my decision.

There was a slight added complication. My employer didn't exactly pay me to check whether my target was worthy of as-sassination. It was a part of the contract, so to speak, that the reason was none of my god damn business.

My mother was the best assassin I have ever seen. My first memories were us training together; she taught me everything she knew, but even with her guidance, I could never be as good as she was. She had something I didn't, you see, a person worth killing for.

Her entire life from the day I was born was about a future for the two of us. Men had been untrustworthy her whole life. She had no respect or time for authorities or the men they represented. She had been abandoned as a baby, and when she had tried to find her family as a young woman, they had been a bitter disappointment.

The voice on the end of the phone had been a lifeline. A way out of the hole she was in and the offer of riches and success. She told me that she had disconnected her job from reality. She didn't remember names, didn't see faces. They were just a number, she was just a tool, a machine, and took no responsibility for the acts she committed. They took her from the orphanage in Russia and trained her to be a ruthless killer. She didn't care about anyone or anything, until me.

She tried to train me in the same way. To remove the responsibility from my shoulders, to see a name as an order number. The last breath nothing more than confirmation the act had been completed. The details were things to take pride in, to show my success and ability. It didn't matter the who, only the how.

I loved the how, brandished it, thrived in the details. I liked the complex killings, a killing of beauty, which showed I was the best in the game. I added my flair and flamboyancy and took delight in pissing all the men off that wanted me dead for daring to show them how a woman could do it better. Good luck finding me.

My mother and I were a formidable duo. A pair that worked together seamlessly while I was a teenager. I brought youth and extravagance, she brought knowledge and experience. I could read her thoughts from the way her body was angled; I knew where she would move before her foot did. Her only fault was that she had me, a liability, but it didn't take long for me to turn into an asset. A young girl with blue eyes and blonde hair could lure anyone, could sneak anywhere, and was the perfect diversion. As I grew so did our tactics. We pushed the limits, took bigger, harder jobs; we were unstoppable.

Until. We weren't.

I took my revenge on my mother's killer. I didn't hunt him down. I instead worked my way through the list of anyone and everyone he may have held dear at any point in his life. I showed no mercy. There was no flounce, it wasn't a job. It was justice. Each one shot with a single bullet. Clean. Efficient. Cold.

It is, to some, my best work. To me, it wasn't working, not a job, it was retribution. He tried to hunt me, as I circled closer, inching my way to the people he really cared about. His brother, his mother, his wife, but I was unstoppable, untraceable, and better than him in every way.

My only complaint was that at the end he welcomed his death. I had taken everything from him, he didn't even beg to live. I wanted that satisfaction, but I didn't lose any sleep over the fact that he had nothing left in his miserable existence so that death was the last relief and comfort. I had tried to make a sport of it. Offered him the chance to escape through the wooded area his house backed onto, but he didn't even run. Just knelt and waited for the whistle of my bullet, so I gave him the slow bleed. Just nicked his heart so he had to experience the slow death, feeling his heart broken, hemorrhaging blood that his brain so vitally needed until his pulse ached in his veins with bloodless pumps.

It seemed like a fitting end, but it had left me a little doubtful of my career path after. The coldness and detachment my mother held was not my strongest point. My moral compass ran on a code. Bad people deserved to die. Good people didn't. Luckily most people are assholes and the planet is better off without them. Especially in these kinds of circles—drugs, politics, crime rings—I could find it easy to justify a killing because the world would be a lot better off without them.

Katherine Scott-Webb didn't fall into that box. In fact, every sign pointed to her being a woman that I actually admired. I had an intrigue; I wanted to know her. I wanted to understand her and I even wanted her to finish her book and take down her abusive ex husband.

So, I had to make a decision. I was either going to kill Katherine Scott-Webb or save her life and protect her. There could be no in-between. I knew if I refused the job, they would task someone else with it. Either way, the target ends up dead. This is why this conversation with Daniel Scott-Webb had become one of the most important of perhaps his whole life.

I had some questions for him and I would know instantly if he were lying.

*"This train for the Manchester Piccadilly is approaching its final destination. This train will terminate here. Thank you for traveling with Virgin Trains. Please note smoking is not permitted at this station."* The loudspeaker sent out its shrill announcement and I gave a soft sigh as I stretched in my tiny seat.

I hoped Daniel Scott-Webb was ready for me.

I HAD ARRANGED a meeting with him under the guise of an internship interview for him. As there were a few variable outcomes, it was important that I was not recognized, so my outfit was an all-out production. I had aged myself a good ten years and went for the dullest, most boring outfit I could find in Marks and Spencer's that screamed *dull office woman*. I wanted to be easily forgotten but with a kind face that would get Daniel Scott-Webb to feel comfortable in opening up to me.

I had made plans to have our meeting at a café that was known for business meetings in the city so it would be totally normal to meet there and not in my office. I took a seat near the window where the sun would gleam through directly in Daniel Scott-Webb's eyes, making it harder for him to focus on my features, because if he was at all like his mother, he had an eye for the details.

I was surprised when he entered. His lack of social media presence made me think he would be unattractive, perhaps overweight or at the very least shy in his appearance. Daniel Scott-Webb was none of these things, and if I had the slightest inclination to sleep with a man, I had a feeling he would be exactly the type I may choose.

He was tall with dark brown hair that looked messy but the sexy kind. His outfit was very appropriate for our meeting: dark fitted pants, a shirt, but then the top button was undone with no tie, which gave an air of casualness. He looked like his father in stature but had the softness of his mother's features, which resulted in a likeability.

He found me instantly and made his way over with a warm smile. I rose with an exaggerated brush down of my awful skirt before I pushed up my glasses and gave a lopsided smile.

"Daniel Scott-Webb?" I questioned as we both sat and he nodded.

"Ms. Buckingham?" he replied as he gestured for a coffee, then looked at me with an inquisitive glance. "Coffee?"

"I will take a tea," I responded in my perfectly clipped English accent.

Once we dealt with pleasantries and we were both settled, I pulled out my notebook and a bunch of papers that looked very official. I watched Daniel Scott-Webb sit up slightly in his seat with an eagerness that showed his youth.

"You come highly recommended for an internship with us. As I am sure you are aware, we do our homework very thoroughly and firstly all cards on the table, we know who your father is and who he looks set to become. Where do you stand in terms of your political alliance and will this be affected by your personal bias?" I watched as Daniel Scott-Webb's eyebrows rose upwards; I didn't dance around the issue and it seemed as though he was not used to that.

"Well, I appreciate your candor and directness. Firstly, I don't hide who my father is but I also don't publicize it and I certainly don't use it for my own gain. If I were accepted on your internship, I would want it to be based on my own merits and achievements not who my father is, or my mother for that matter."

I liked that he referenced her.

"As for my political bias, I do not have one. I wish my father the best of success in his endeavors, but he does not play an active role in my life, and nor do I in his. The person who has shaped my life and my political persuasions is, in fact, my mother, and I think you will find that she aligns very much with your own so I don't think that will be a problem, but I can outlay some of the areas if you would like?"

It was my turn to lean forwards; Daniel Scott-Webb was a great conveyer. I had no doubt he would make a great politician himself, and I was beginning to wonder if this was the true drive behind his Reddit persona. His marketplace to grow that audience.

"And what about your mother's book?"

His silence was deafening and I felt the tingles of adrenaline. I wasn't dancing around the subject; I was diving in and the ball was in his court. Maybe he would deny, maybe he would hide, maybe he wouldn't answer. I glanced over my glasses, my fingers reaching for the handle of my cup of tea, leaving the silence so he was forced to take his step. He weighed his options; I watched his brain click through them. The challenge arose—he wanted to question me, but he wanted the job more.

"I support my mother 100 percent in everything she does. She is an exemplary role model to anyone and an exceptional human being. I don't wish to discuss it further than that."

Bingo.

## 5

I almost felt bad that I couldn't offer Daniel Scott-Webb an internship. He really deserved one but in fact, although he didn't know it, he had just saved his mother's life, which in the grand scheme of things I think he should take as a win. The train back to London was highly uneventful and just as uncomfortable, but it did give me a little time to think about my next move.

I toyed with some different options. I could kidnap Katherine Scott-Webb, this would mean I wouldn't have to tell her who I was, and then just get her to write the rest of her story while locked in the basement or something. There were some definite risks associated with this plan though, and I wasn't sure I would be promoting the best working environment.

The next option would be to tell her the truth and hope by some miracle she kept her cool and calmly accompanied me out of the country. Again, I could see some elements of risk. For example, who would actually trust their hired hitman to escort them out of their home and into an undisclosed off-grid location?

I supposed my only real option would be a half-truth, half-hidden-truth disclosure. I would need to show Katherine Scott-Webb that she was in danger, and prove to her that I was, in fact, on her side. She would already recognize me; of that I was sure. So, it would now be a case of explaining to her that her husband knew exactly what she was doing, someone has been sent to kill her and without me, they would almost certainly succeed.

I didn't need to tell her that I had been sent to kill her in the first place but by a strange twist of fate I would now become her protector.

This seemed like the best plan to me. There would be no way that Katherine Scott-Webb could know my real initial purpose. She would trust that her husband knew and would in turn be more aware than me of the lengths he would go to silence her.

The question now was what was the best approach in delivering this news. Well, of course, subtlety was my specialty...

I SAT in the dark in the center of Katherine Scott-Webb's lounge. What can I say? I do love a bit of theatre. I had moved the armchair so I was positioned directly central so whichever way she entered she would see me sitting in an unthreatening position. I had worn soft colors and tried to look as inoffensive and as meek as possible.

In hindsight, I should have perhaps not been waiting in her home at 10 pm at night, and instead rather knocked on the door once she had arrived. But I didn't care for hindsight all that much and I was still El. She let herself in and bustled around in the hallway, peeling off her shoes and dropping her bag on the side counter. She let out a deep sigh and I heard the snap of her bra as she freed herself from its restraints.

I thought she would come straight into the lounge but instead, she veered off to the kitchen and I head the fridge open and the soft pop of a cork as she poured herself a large glass of perfectly chilled chardonnay. I could almost taste the crisp dryness on my tongue although I wasn't really a dry white wine kind of woman. Predictably for a russian, I liked vodka—short, sharp and direct to the point, but she made me hungry for a taste.

She flicked the living room switch and as the light came on, she froze in the door frame. The panic was instant and she physically recoiled in fear and then her eyes recognized my features, a flicker of remembrance and it seemed to calm her a little.

"I know you." Her voice had an edge of fear but was clear.

"Yes, we met, at the restaurant."

"And now you are in my home. What do you want?"

Her confidence grew with each word, her body language changing. I could see her now braless nipples hard through the sheen of her pale pink satin dress. Her skin had a soft flush as blood pounded through her veins. The act of fight or flight mode was very much activated and at odds with each other, which left her body alert.

"I need to tell you some information and once I have, we need to move quickly. I can answer more after, but time is of the essence and you will need to listen to me very carefully. Do you understand?" Her eyes widened a fraction and her fingers tightened around the stem of her glass. She paused, taking in a long deep breath, her options flickering through her mind. I saw her eye the phone, the door, the window. If I had wanted it so, she could be dead before she even made a choice of where to move.

"Okay. Tell me," she said after a second and then drained her glass in one swift fluid movement; she set her empty glass on the shelf and I swear she glanced for a coaster. These rich women never ceased to amaze me.

"I know what you are writing. I know

what you are saying and I know that you are telling the truth. The problem is that I am not the only one who knows. I would like you to finish, I think it should be published and Britain should know the kind of man they are about to elect into office. Unfortunately, there are others who know about the book who do not feel the same way."

It was good she had let go of her glass, as I watched her nails dig so deep into her palms, I was sure she would draw blood. If I thought I had alarmed Katherine Scott-Webb with my presence it was nothing compared to the deathly paleness that rose in her like fear grasping at her heart.

"James knows?" Two words, and if I had any doubt before as to whether she was telling the truth, there certainly wasn't any now. She looked like a scared little girl as she crumbled before me.

"Yes, Katherine, he knows. If you come with me, I will protect you."

It is moments like this that define us. Katherine had a choice to make. She could bury her head in the sand and wait for her imminent death to come knocking. Or, she could come with me and dive into the un-known. The pause was merely a second; she was, after all, a fighter.

"I will put some things together." She turned and headed up the stairs. I watched as her bare toes curled in the plush, creamy carpets and I had a sudden urge to lick the pearlescent skin of her ankle bone. She stopped as though she heard my thoughts. She barely turned, her eyes just glancing back to meet mine as she asked me quizzi-cally, "What is your name?"

"Elena. But you can call me El."

And so, our getaway began.

I TRIED to keep my excitement under wraps but I was like a kid in a candy shop. If Katherine Scott- Webb was expecting a professional escape exit CIA-style, with a black mercedes and men in suits, she was going to be hugely disappointed as that just didn't appeal to my tastes.

We needed to get out of London, cross the channel into France, and from there make our way to my chateau. Getting out of

London would seem easy, there were hundreds of transport links that we could network through, but the next guy to come for Katherine Scott-Webb would be another professional and we really needed to cover our tracks meticulously.

"We need to change your appearance," I said to her and she nodded her consent to me.

As I started to pin her hair up into a cap, getting her ready for the blonde wig I was about to fit for her, I started to ask her questions. They were just about her movements, who would notice her missing, how she travelled usually, who could cover for her so an absence wouldn't draw too much attention, especially in the early days.

The good thing about my creative kills meant Katherine disappearing wouldn't throw up a red flag for a couple of days. My employer would assume that I had gotten imaginative, and that bought us around 48 hours before questions would be asked.

Once I had gripped the blonde bob wig in place, I turned her to look at me, being just a few inches away from Katherine's face gave me an intimate view of her features. There were soft lines of age that kissed her skin but that's all they were, feathery touches of wisdom that only enhanced her features. Her eyes shone bright with a steely determination and her jaw was set with a firm resolute. She reminded me of a warrior, a shieldmaiden, a Viking heroine with a fierce heart that had been overlooked before but never again.

My hand rose slowly, instinctively. I had no control. I just wanted to touch her skin, to feel her warmth, and offer her comfort. She was terrified, scared, and felt alone. Except she wasn't alone, she was with me, and whilst I could not promise a boring escape plan, I could give her my word that I would do all I could to keep her safe.

"Close your eyes," I murmured and she followed my direction. I swear her lips puckered and for a second I felt myself lean closer—I could feel her breath against my skin—and then I swiped the brush over her eyelid. A slow sweep of a dark grey powder, much darker than she would ever normally wear, but of course it suited her, in a clash against her soft femininity.

Katherine Scott-Webb intrigued me, I

breathed in her expensive perfume and watched as she gave herself into my care, I felt an odd feeling sweep through me. I could slit her throat now, it would take a second, she would be breathing her last breaths before her eyes even opened. But my instincts cried in revolt. They wanted only to protect her.

She could be my savior or my biggest mistake, only time would tell.

## 6

---

**W**ork El kicked in. Everything my mother had taught me came into play. I needed to be on the top of my game and I felt it tingle through my veins. With new hair, essentials packed and the security disabled, we left Katherine's house through the back. I knew more or less exactly how to avoid the immediate cameras as I would have done had I actually gone through with killing her, but as we headed more into street CCTV we would, for sure, be captured on film.

I had to make a choice, together or not. The longer my boss didn't know I was helping Katherine, the more time it would buy us. But that meant coaching her to a level I just didn't have time for. So, I made a choice. From the very first cam sighting, they would know I had turned. It would put me on the list, a thought that both excited me and scared me in equal measures because one thing was for sure, it was not a list with a prize for winning.

Katherine had the composure of a woman who had been in the spotlight and used to extreme pressure. She listened attentively to my instructions and with an air of determined grit stepped up to the plate. She was physically in great shape—Pilates and jogging according to her calendar—and she kept the pace as we made our way down the streets.

We had needed black to get out of her garden and cut across the neighbors, but two women moving quickly, all in black with duffel bags would draw attention on brightly lit London streets. So, we had ditched the dark coats and revealed comfortable clothes that didn't seem out of place for a couple of friends taking a night coach down to the coast for a few days.

At the bus station, I bought two tickets

with cash at the machine and two at the kiosk. We then took a black cab for our actual trip. They were old tricks, subtle diversions. Nothing that would throw a professional off, but it would buy us a few minutes, cause a stumble, and if we kept throwing enough of them, we had more chance of making it to the chateau without being traced.

It took 48 minutes between leaving Katherine's house and us sitting in the black cab on the way to the south coast. The hatch between us and the driver was closed. The sound transfer to the front of the cab was switched off. She reached for her phone on instinct before remembering. I had taken it from her wiped it and given it to a homeless person. Destroying the phone would be a red flag. Her phone still on, pinging a signal, and in use would be less of a red flag.

She sat by the window in the back of the cab next to me and laid her head against the glass with a light sigh. She looked tired, exhausted, and it was only 11 pm. This was only the beginning. There were going to be some long days, sleepless nights, and uncertain times ahead.

"Are you okay?" I asked, and her gaze turned to me, I felt those dissecting eyes run over me, but she gave me no answer. I leaned back in my chair; chin tilted upwards in almost a defiant stance. I wasn't here to be analyzed by Katherine Scott-Webb.

"I am worried for my son. James will not harm him, but he can make his life difficult. He will think Daniel knows something and Daniel will be worried sick. Someone was asking questions already; he was spooked today but I didn't speak to him properly to get more details."

I didn't volunteer that the someone was me. I felt the less she knew about how I arrived in her lounge the better.

"We will let Daniel know you are safe when you are safe. Until then... he should be worried and cautious. Your ex-husband may not want to hurt Daniel, but I imagine a few months ago, he didn't want you assassinated either. Daniel is smart, I am sure he will keep himself safe."

She nodded. "He is and he will. So, now, we make our way to the south?"

"Yes, we need to cross the channel but I haven't a concrete idea on how yet. I tend to find that these things will often present themselves with solutions." I reached in the duffle and pulled out a tube of Pringles, I popped the top and took a noisy crunch before I offered Katherine the tube. She shook her head and I gave her a shrug, tucking in more.

"What happens then?"

"Well," I replied through my crunches, "I have a safe house. Once we get there, you will need to write. Finish what you started. I don't know how long that will take you but the quicker the better. Once the book is published, the risk to you drops hugely. You have no value as a target then. We will set up some fail safes too, you know, just in case, but I am certain once we get you into safety your husband and his hired hands won't be able to touch you. It is getting there quickly and undetected that poses the biggest complications. But you are smart, you know the alternative. I am confident on our chances. I'm a professional."

We pulled up at traffic lights and a guy on the street tried to approach the window of the cab.

"Fuck off, asshole," my tone warranted no argument.

Katherine raised her perfectly plucked eyebrows and I rolled my eyes. "I thought we were going undetected," she whispered softly with a slight smile curling at the corner of her lips.

"I don't like assholes," I mumbled with a shrug. "It is a perfectly acceptable thing. Some people are just fucking idiots."

"You sound like a child," Katherine replied and leaned over brushing the crumbs from my shirt. Her fingers are slim, delicate, and they moved with a soft caring touch and I felt my heart beat a little faster.

I don't like labels, I wouldn't say for example that I was gay, a lesbian, even bisexual. I think of my sexuality as more fluid. About a person, a feeling, a moment. OK, so generally I have those feelings and moments with people who are women, but I still don't like the label. I have enjoyed men, but they didn't offer me any further satisfaction than a one-night thrill—oh, who was I kidding, it was more of an hour at best.

Women, on the other hand, were tantalizing and the more difficult they were to read the more I wanted them. I spend my days figuring people out, dissecting them, learning about their lives from the way they walk, talk, breathe. If I find a woman who holds a secret, who I can't unravel... I am lost in her charm. That is until I figure her out, solve the puzzle, and then I move on. It has always worked for me, they had a good time; pretty things, attention, mind-blowing sex, and then I was gone and they would never find me again. Nobody can disappear like I can. Everyone wins.

But Katherine Scott-Webb is not a huge mystery to me. I have unwrapped her life relatively easily. I have glimpsed into the darkest times of her life, read her fears, her pain, her heartache in her own words. I know the scars she wears on the outside as well as the ones inside.

It wasn't that I wanted to figure her out. It wasn't that, at all. So, what was it?

I watched her fall into a light sleep. Her blonde wig irritating her scalp so her fingers were drawn there like a magnet, tangling in the synthetic hair as her breath painted condensation along the tinted glass window of the cab.

The lights of the motorway passed at the same intervals, shining across her face, lighting up her pale skin with a flicker before it was gone. I found myself waiting for them, to kiss her features with their light touch. She really was beautiful, vulnerable but with this steely grit that I couldn't help but admire.

The cab driver hit a pothole and her head thudded against the glass. I thought it would wake her, but it didn't. Instead, she lightly rolled her neck and her head fell against my shoulder. She nuzzled in and found the soft spot where she could rest in the nape of my neck, and I let her lie like that until we arrived at the coast.

---

## 7

"Is it really necessary to check into three different hotels?" Katherine muttered under her breath as we made our way over to the elevator. It was the first hint of discontent I had heard from her all day, and it had been a long day.

We got out the cab at separate points and I gave a plan to Katherine. Having time to map out a rendezvous point with Katherine this time, we could be more careful, and she had followed it perfectly. She had checked in the first, me the second, and now together at the third, with a change of clothes and wigs.

She was currently a redhead; I was

blonde but brassier, and I had acquired a French accent that I was rather fond of. Katherine was too although she didn't say it out loud; I just felt her approval as I asked in my broken English to make a reservation for two days longer than we needed.

As the doors pinged and we stepped in to the elevator, she grinned at me. "Maybe I could do an accent though. I think I would like that. I felt very Bonnie and Clyde in the last place when I left through the service door."

"Well, I hope you didn't feel *too* Bonnie and Clyde. They didn't exactly have the ending I am hoping for."

Katherine looked at me and then let out a light giggle and I couldn't help myself, I grinned too. Maybe it was sleep deprivation, the crash of adrenaline, the thrill of the run but as the doors reopened on our floor, we were both laughing hysterically. So much so that I could barely get the key card in the slot. We fell into our perfectly made room and collapsed on the bed.

"Why are you doing this?" Her voice was barely audible, but of course I heard her. I took a soft breath and turned on the mattress to face her, brassy blonde hair fanning out across crisp white sheets.

"Because... people deserve to know the truth. And you don't deserve to die for it. I really believe that, Katherine."

She turned to me, the creases of laughter faded, and her eyes filled with tears. "He will find me eventually." It wasn't a question and she was probably right. James Webb would see Katherine again. Either as a published author who had wrecked his private life and political career or dead on a gurney. I knew which he would prefer, I knew which I would put my money on.

"He might find you, but the circumstances of that... Well, they could not be too favorable to him."

"I don't know why I started writing it." She fell onto her back and stared up at the ceiling. "Just, I saw him inching closer and closer to number 10 Downing Street. Closer and closer to being the most powerful man in this country. He has been painted as this saint, such a great guy, amicable divorce, handsome son, pretty new wife. And I couldn't stand it. I had to just say it, after all these years of carrying it around. So, I started, and then I couldn't stop. Reliving it... it was like therapy, you know. I can't forgive him for what he did to me, but I could start to forgive myself." I watched a single tear run from the corner of her eye.

"I wasn't going to publish. It was Daniel who told me I had to. He said it wasn't fair to the country to let him get elected. I know he is right, but I protected Daniel a lot, well, as much as I could. He was a child, he saw, he knew things, but never the worst and I am thankful for that. But it also means he wouldn't think that we would now be on the run from assassination attempts too. He sees the bad in his father, but not the worst. Do you think he will be safe?"

"Yes, I think that Daniel will know you have gone to ground to finish. He is smart. He will keep his head down and it will all be okay." My hand reached and so did hers, our fingers threaded in a soft hold. I didn't make any other move, just offered her gentle reassurance. "You should rest, Katherine. We have to cross the channel tomorrow and international travel is always the trickiest. We need to be on our A-game." I gave her a soft squeeze then moved away from her. Letting her settle on the bed as I made up the sofa. I swear her eyes lingered, a thought drifted on her lips, but she let it go and with a nod turned away from me, and before long I heard the soft deep breathing of her dreams.

WE BOTH GOT a good rest and ordered in room service; I ate with my normal vigor and love of food and Katherine watched me with a soft smile at every mouthful I devoured. She eats in the same way as she does everything really, with a style normal people could never master. Even eating a half decent burger, she managed to make it look classy, with a light dab of her napkin to the corners of her mouth when the faintest spot of ketchup stained her lips. Me... I had grease running down my fingers. I don't pause for niceties; food is a fuel —but it is also delicious and I enjoy every mouthful.

"Are you ready for the ferry?" she asked

me and as I swallowed my last mouthful, I nodded.

"I can get on no problem. I have a few passports that will let me take the ferry undetected. You are the complication. You are not exactly famous, but you might be recognized by the right person. You have no papers, no docs. So, I need to bribe your way on. Luckily, I know a guy and if he is at the docks, we can get on via the loading bay. From there it will just be as easy as taking the elevator up to the decks, but if he isn't there, it could be trickier. I am not worried though. Most people can be bribed for the right price and I generally know the right price."

"Is there like a school you go to for this kind of thing?" she asked earnestly, and it caught me off guard. I laughed loudly and felt the hint of my Russian accent creep into my sentence. "No, no school. Just life, you learn or you die."

"You never really did explain what you do, or even who sent you."

"I know."

I didn't mean to abruptly end the conversation, but Katherine was walking on dangerous ground and she had to realize that. She did and backtracked instantly.

"Well, however you found me, or whoever sent you, to them I am grateful."

And I felt my first twinge of guilt.

KATHERINE WAS a fast learner with a lot on the line. She embraced the changing identities, the fast pace in which we moved. She added some sass, class when required, and didn't stifle my creativity. If anything, she inspired me to go further and be more.

She slipped on knee-length leather boots, fishnet tights and tucked her hair in the short black bob like she was a professional. She swayed her ass with every step she took along the docks, and when Chuck saw her... he was never going to say no to let us both on for a cash-filled envelope.

She had seven decks to change her outfit and whilst I could do it in two, she impressed me that she even remembered the lipstick change as the fifth pinged past. I knew that these dances were only buying us time. It wasn't until I got into France with her that I could really shake off any trace of our movements, but every minute could make the difference when the hunter began his chase.

It was only midday but we headed for the ferry bar. There wasn't much to do for the next couple of hours and I had a car that we would pick up just outside of Calais, which included a few hours of walking, which I hadn't told Katherine about just yet. So, we might as well enjoy the couped-up tin shell of a ferry.

I had watched Katherine polish off a bottle of wine to little effect. One vodka and her eyes glazed and her lips loosened. "You are very beautiful you know," she told me in a hushed drunken whisper that was actually louder than her normal speaking voice.

"Is that so?" I said with a wry smile. Drunk girls were not my thing, but I did like to hear the thoughts she kept to herself normally.

"Yes... and you know it. I know that you are always trying to..." She pointed her fingers at my eyes and then back to her face wafting up and down, "...read me."

I picked up my own vodka and drained the glass. Just one. It takes the edge off. "What do you think it is that I am trying to read about you?"

"I don't think you even know the answer to that question," she replied truthfully and drained her own glass, mirroring me. My eyebrows rose involuntarily at the accuracy of her statement. She was right.

"Should you really be drinking anyway?" she asked with a swift change in subject. "Aren't you supposed to be driving soon?"

"Well... about that. We may have a little walk..."

*- Seven Hours Later -*

"For goodness's sake, El! Is it much further?!"

When I stored the car five hours from the ferry port, it was an Elena five hours. An upbeat, focused jog. My mother had taught me how important it was to have these routes, these backups, these fail-safes because you just didn't know when you might need it. Now though, with Katherine, the terrain was unfamiliar to her. She was generally fit but a five-hour jog at a constant pace took weeks, months, of training. So, we had to walk, and we got slower. And slower. And slower.

Even I was getting fed up so I could imagine for her it seemed like some slow torture.

"Would you like to play a game?" I asked, and I heard her sigh.

"You know sometimes you are really a high-functioning adult and others you are like a child. No, I don't want to play a game! I want to get to this bloody car and rest my feet. I should have had more vodka." She added the last part under her breath and I couldn't help but laugh, and even in the setting sun, I could see the smile spread on her face.

As twigs snapped under our shoes and the leaves rustled ominously in the darkening skies, we made our way closer. We weren't far now and we would be back on the road again. I could get us to the Chateau in a few hours if I drove there directly but I would detour. Take a couple of days. I wouldn't put Aveline and Kit at risk in any way.

Plus, it wasn't much of a French road

trip if we didn't even stay in a hotel or fancy B&B. As we reached the clearing, the apparently disused warehouse came into view. It was security monitored and my storage space had been paid for ten years. Places like this, they dealt with people like me. "Wait here," I said softly to Katherine and I jogged the last half mile, knowing she could keep me in her vision and it would ease any panic at being left.

I slipped through the gap in the fence then made my way to the shutter door and entered my keycode. The doors slid open and I made my way to my lot, my little fiat was there in the same place as I left her. My fingers trailed under the wheel trim and I unclipped the keys from their hiding place.

Within two minutes I was driving out of the warehouse and round the back lane to pick up Katherine. I felt a sense of control behind the wheel, more options available. There was money, plates, guns in the back, and the regained feeling of control bought me a feeling of calm and clarity.

Katherine Scott-Webb was not my partner. She was my job. Not even a paid job anymore. A passion project. Either way, I had let her into my head and thoughts and desires and I needed to stop letting her in there because she was clouding my judgment.

I pulled up alongside her and she almost fell into the passenger seat. In seconds she had slipped her sneakers from her toes and was massaging her aching feet. As I changed gear and glanced at the stick, I caught a view of her ankle, pale soft skin aching after a long, long day. Katherine Scott-Webb was definitely clouding my judgment, and the real truth was I really liked it.

## 8

"**R**abinovich?"

At the corner of Grove Street was a man who looked completely out of place in upper-class Belgravia. He hovered, in his dark coat with short dark hair and eyes that had an ominous stare.

"Yes." His response wasn't a question, but it was a statement and a cold one at that. The caller was wasting his time and Rabinovich didn't like to have his time wasted. He liked to get on with the job in hand.

He knew that Elena was not made of the same grit as her mother had been. Now *she* was a fine Russian. A thoroughbred killing machine. A work he could respect, even admire. El, the girl? He wrinkled his nose in distaste. She was all about the show, liked to leave her calling card, liked to be remembered. It was not the name of the game. It wasn't how it was played, and it was the opposite of Russian. Assassins were meant to be forgotten, just like the people they killed. It was supposed to be quiet, hushed up. Not flounced and displayed.

It was only a matter of time before she fucked up. And this smelt of a fuck up.

"What have you found?" asked the voice on the end of the line.

"Nothing," Rabinovich replied, his voice terse.

"No dead body? No Elena?"

"Nothing," Rabinovich repeated.

"I don't understand." This Rabinovich could agree with though he kept quiet until the voice issued a low, resigned sigh. "Fine. Just... get me some answers and quickly. They need to be found, both of them. What an absolute fuck up, she better have a—" Rabinovich ended the call. He didn't need to hear the frustrated ramblings of his paycheck. He needed to do his job, and right now his job seemed to be less killing and more hunting.

And Rabinovich was good at hunting.

AFTER THE FOURTH loop around I decided we could stop at the Fleur Èpanouie Hotel as long as they let me pay cash for a suite. Some hotels now liked to have a credit card swiped when securing one of the larger rooms, and a credit card swipe was like having a huge flashing sign in the sky saying: *ELENA AND KATHERINE SCOTT–WEBB ARE STAYING HERE!!!*

Not ideal.

Especially as we were both exhausted because we had already driven for hours and hours and hours in circles, loops, crossovers, and diversions. I was beginning to think even I was acting a little paranoid.

"Bonjour, Mademoiselle. Souhaitez-vous faire une réservation avec nous?" asked the pretty blonde at reception, and I replied to her in fluent and perfect French.

I told her that I would like a suite, two

nights, cash. She nodded without so much as a raised perfectly plucked eyebrow.

"Ce sera 1200€" I didn't flinch, I simply paid with a faux smile and took my key.

Katherine entered thirty minutes later, changed into clothes I had stashed in the car. She headed straight for the lift where I join her from the lobby as though by chance. I pressed the button for six and she didn't move, just let me take us where we needed to be.

As I opened the hotel room door, I knew a suite was the right choice.

A queen bed dominated the room but the couch looked like it would be like a cloud to lay on. The sheets were crisp and fresh, the towels thick and fluffy. The tub was oversized and made for bubbles and soaking, which was exactly what I needed, but first...

I pulled out the emergency pack from my bag that includes some maps, transport data, cash, pick-up points. I laid the map out across the floor and found our exact location. My brain whirred into action. The process at this point is hard to describe, it is like my brain is following the patterns, the possible routes, possible issues, cameras, checkpoints, risks.

I allocated a point to each risk and began to rate them. I know from this current location there are six possible routes to the chateau. None are perfect, but they all have merits and cause for concern. I would guess that questions were being asked now. My silence was the first red flag, the lack of a body the second. If someone hadn't been sent to Katherine Scott-Webb's house yet, one would be there shortly, and I could only hope that the dance up until this point would buy us enough time to get home.

Katherine dropped to the floor beside me. "Are you okay? You must be exhausted," she murmured and her hands reached for my temples. It was the gentlest of touches, barely a glance against my skin, but I felt my body respond.

I looked to her; my eyes searched her face as hers did mine. Questions were left unasked, and most definitely unanswered, but at that moment, it didn't seem to matter.

She was my prey. I was her hunter. Yet

now, I felt like I was the one who was caught.

I leaned forwards onto my knees, paper ruffles and creases beneath me but I didn't care. The tips of my fingers curled under the edge of her wig. I didn't want her to be anyone else other than Katherine. She sat perfectly still, letting me free her dark brown glossy curls before she shook them out with a light roll of her neck.

"Is this okay?" My hand cupped her face tenderly. I wouldn't normally ask, I would know, but I felt with Katherine that I needed her to be sure, needed her to want this as much as I do.

"I don't... I am not very... I don't know how..." My fingers traced her jawline, my index finger resting at her lips with a light shush.

"That doesn't matter. I just need to know... is this okay? Do you want this? Me? Me touching you. Is this ok?" She paused a moment, yet it seemed to last minutes, hours, days and then she nodded.

Both of my hands moved, cupping her face, caressing her soft skin. I tilted her chin up, angling her lips to mine and I leaned in, dipped into her space, and I took my first kiss. She smelled like expensive Chanel and tasted like heaven. My tongue lingered along her lower lip, tracing, trailing before she parted them for me and I could really stake my claim.

As her lips pressed, my tongue darted for a long leisurely swirl, tasting her, and as her tongue met mine, I lifted my chin, just an inch, lips parting so I could suck her tongue softly. It was a dirty kiss, filled with a lust that built and rose in me like an inextinguishable fire.

My fingers slid back into her hair and I guided her backward onto the hotel floor. Her lovely hair fanned across the thick carpet, as my lips left hers, only moving to her chin, her neck so I could pepper her soft creamy skin in light lingering kisses.

My teeth trailed along the pulsing vein in her neck and my tongue licked her skin, tasting her. I felt her pulse hammering underneath my tongue, her body awakened, alive, bursting with lust as I moved with a gentle yet wanting need.

I moved my hands down her body, my fingertips tracing over her soft curves, rising over her breasts then dipping down along her slim waist. I traced circles around her navel, inching lower and lower to the hem of her silk shirt. My silk shirt. I took the edges between my finger and thumb and I pulled upwards, slowly, unwrapping her like the perfect present on Christmas day. She looked up at me with trusting eyes, her eyes looked dark with lust as she gave herself to me.

My head dropped, each inch I revealed, my mouth followed with kisses against her warmth. Along her hip bone, circling her belly button, up and across her ribs, my nose traced over the middle of her bra and my tongue licked the valley between her breasts. I heard her gasp...her hands reached upwards as she stretched herself out for me, offering me more of her, which I gladly took.

Her back arched and I pulled her shirt up, over her face, and pulled it off over her long dark hair. My kisses never paused—I couldn't get enough of her. I could feel her shyness, her body responded but her mind was hesitant, unsure how to react and respond.

"Katherine," I murmured against her skin as my tongue lingered over the swell of her breasts. "Relax. There are no rules. Just enjoy. Touch where you want. Move how you want. No. Rules."

She took a light breath and nodded softly, but I didn't give her time to over-think. Instead, I started to undress myself, not naked, just stripping to my Calvin Klein sports bra and panties. I didn't want to overwhelm her, but I needed her to see how much I desired her, how much I wanted her, and the spreading wet line down the center of my panties was a clear indication of how turned on she made me.

Her fingers rose with a light tremble and then they ran over my body tracing the contours of my faint muscles. I am fit, in shape but not overly defined. Just the light outline of abs, a six-pack hinted at but not quite there.

I went still, letting her fingers linger, they spread against my waist and then pushed upwards, skimming over my breast, exploring, learning, knowing.

My knees parted and rested on either side of her thighs and I took down her pants; she lifted her ass up and they rode over the curve of her cheeks, down her legs, over her knees then I let them fall down her calves before she shook them free from her ankles.

My fingers ran up her shins and pushed her knees apart, they fell open, she looked nervous as I slipped between them as easily as though I had always been there. She rested up on her elbows and watched me as I dipped between her thighs and buried my face against her pussy. I breathed her in through the black lace, taking in her smell, her heat, feeling the throb of her sex against my tongue as I licked over the fabric, ravenous like an animal, for even the lightest of tastes. She was as turned on as I was. Her body was speaking for her.

She let out a tiny whimper and I began to bite, my teeth grazing over her flushed folds beneath the lace until I could grip it. I tugged with a hard pull and slowly she bared herself for me.

She was trimmed neatly- of course she was, I had studied her schedule, she had a regular appointment for a wax- and my tongue ran down her velvety wetness with one deep swipe. Her response was instant, her back arched, and her shoulders scraped down the carpet, which I knew would redden her skin, which really fucking turned me on.

I know how to please women; I know how to make them writhe for me, but with Katherine it was different. I don't just want a cheap thrill; I want to take her higher, I want her to enjoy each wave, each touch, each moment.

So, I paused after each move I made to see how she responded, to see what she liked, what she loved, what made her toes curl and her head spin with dizzying pleasure. My head dipped lower and I pointed my tongue so I could circle her entrance nice and slow. I teased her wider, feeling a drip of her lust on my tongue, and her taste exploded in my mouth.

My face moved upwards, my tongue trailing up to her clit. I flicked over it lightly, over and over, up and down, left to right. I took it in my mouth and sucked. It drove her wild, her nails raked the carpet and her hips bucked whilst she thrust her hips upwards to meet my eager mouth. I brought my right hand up and pushed two fingers inside of her, curling the tips as I did so. Her moans grew louder, her entire body vibrating with an urgency as her orgasm prepared to overtake her.

"Fuck, El... I—Oh...Oh... Don't stop ..."

*She says 'fuck' during sex.*

Like I had any intention of stopping. Her breasts were held by the tight confines of her bra as sweat glistened on her skin. The louder she moaned, the faster my mouth moved, the harder my fingers thrust until I pushed her to the point of no control. I felt her tighten, her pulse throbbing against my tongue, before her wetness flooded against my palm and lips.

I thought about not stopping, just continuing and pushing her through her first orgasm and straight into the second. But I also wanted her to enjoy it, to enjoy each rippling wave, those moments where you start to catch your breath and the world begins to come into focus once more. I wanted to give her that.

So, I cupped her sex and let her press against me, her most intimate place held in my warmth. Her breath began to slow but her body still shook, soft low murmurs escaped from her lips as she sunk into the carpet and floated back down to earth.

"Are you okay?" I asked lightly as I crawled beside her. I gave her no space to move away, rather pulling her into my arms and embrace, holding her tight against me.

"I am... something," she replied with a shy smile.

I would take something.

# 9

"**R**abinovich?"

"Yes," he replied tersely as he leaned over some street CCTV footage. He was almost too surprised to answer at the charade that was playing out in front of him. Little Elena and Katherine Scott-Webb. Oh, how his employer was not going to like this update; he might even smile at the development if that were something he ever did.

"Is she dead?" the caller asked.

"She?" he asked with little thought given to the speaker, instead much more focused on the security feed.

"Yes. She," the voice repeated with

rising frustration, he really hated dealing with Rabinovich. Every word, question, and update was like pulling teeth and his lack of patience poured into every word he spoke.

"Which she?" Rabinovich asked as he leaned closer, enlarging the frame as a trembling Katherine stepped into a black cab. He had the licence plate. He could trace the cab.

"Any she!" the caller replied with heated frustration. "Katherine. El. She. Her. Both. Any. Either!"

"No. Neither are dead," he replied as he watched them drive off. He pulled up further security footage as he tried to track the cab.

"Well, then what the fuck is going on?!"

"They left London together. Would you like me to trace them?"

"Together?" he spluttered. "They left togeth—would I like you to trace them? Of course, I would like you to trace them! What do you think I am paying you for? You find them and then you kill the target and then. Well, then... I will deal with Elena." He cut the line, which saved Rabinovich the job; he did not sound happy.

Rabinovich, on the other hand, was very pleased with himself. He finally had a chance to hunt down that jumped up little girl Elena who thought she could play with the big boys and show her how real Russian assassins worked.

I WOKE WITH A LAZY, just-fucked freshness that tingled through my body. Which is exactly what had happened. Katherine may not be experienced with women, nothing more than a few college fumbles and French kisses apparently, but once the fire had been lit it didn't take long for me to coax her out of her shyness.

I didn't want to overwhelm her, to make her feel like she didn't know how to pleasure a woman because the truth was, with a little guidance, patience and intent, anyone could pleasure a woman. She gave me her fingers, her lips and her tongue with such wide-eyed eagerness that made even the lightest of touches resonate deep within me.

We barely left the hotel floor all night, only after hours of learning each other's bodies, to curl up in the sheets, upon which we decided to get reacquainted all over again. I had been nervous, which I never was, as the morning approached. There was something about the fresh light of a new day that could cast shadows on even the most wondrous of nights.

But Katherine had woken to no such reservations. Only questions. It seemed she now had to know every single thing about me and what I did and who I was, and this was infinitely more difficult for me to navigate than an actual minefield.

"I need to clear my mind and think, Katherine. I can't be playing twenty questions now, I have to keep you safe," I had replied in mock sternness as I spread my maps and papers out once more.

She pulled the sheets around her and leaned in, watching me from under smudged eye make up and messy bed hair. "Explain it to me."

"There isn't that much to explain really,

it is just that I need to figure out the best route for us. There are options. I made options based on a few scenarios. The only problem..." I paused and Katherine sighed, rolling her eyes for dramatic effect.

"I am a CEO, I understand the use of the word *problem* in this context. I am a problem. Not me personally. Not I, Katherine Scott-Webb, but the fact that I am an additional person." I smiled at her.

"Yes, you are my problem. Sexy ..." As I began each word, I leaned in closer to her and began to trail kisses along her jaw. "... Smart ... Beautiful ... Wonderful ..." Hovering at her lips I whispered, "... but still a problem."

"Well, how do we solve the problem," she replied with a sexy husk. I paused. My body was responding to her and my thoughts were already between her legs. But my head was more rational, thinking, fired up and ready to go. Not to mention, the overwhelming thought of *there will be more sex if we both survive the next few days.*

And that was undeniable logic.

"Okay. Well, we have to balance a few different things. I give us 72 hours before we are traced into France. That could be optimistic so I will say 48 to be on the safe side. So, time is definitely a considerable factor. Next is the skill set of the person trailing is, and it will be high. The highest, maybe even Rabinovich—not that I think he is the best- I am the best- but in the absence of me, he is definitely a worthy adversary. I digress, the next point boils down to things that are not completely relevant in this case although I do think that keeping the level of causalities down should be a priority," I rambled, only to pause at the look on Katherine's face.

"Yes," she stuttered, "I would say that was a priority."

"Exactly. So, all those things considered, option four is our best plan."

And so, option four began.

OF COURSE, it wasn't the simplest of plans. It included some cycling through the French countryside, two-car changes, a night bus, a loop around Leon for no reason other than to lose ourselves again if we had been detected, and then the last trip to the chateau involved the final car journey and a full day hike.

Katherine took each leg in her stride, her confidence growing with each hurdle we overcame. France is a beautiful country, full of stunning countryside, hearty wines, and delicious food. There were moments when we both lost sight of the danger and instead just enjoyed the moments we had together.

My job didn't come with a sit-back-and-relax, four-weeks-paid vacation a year. Katherine, as a CEO, wasn't someone who took time off either. I am not sure which of us needed it more, but we gripped the freedom with both hands.

I laughed as mud splattered up our backs as we cycled along the river Saône, and Katherine couldn't breathe for laughter when my wheel hitting a hole sent me headfirst into the bushes. We peppered the miles with kisses, touches, flirtatious glances, and explorations of each other's bodies and minds.

Luckily my real job and my current saving-Katherine job seemed to have blended in her mind that I worked as some kind of secret operative, which wasn't wrong. The wrong part would be the side on which I batted for. Katherine saw me as her hero whereas, in reality, I was the villain.

She took it well that I didn't want to talk about my job so we instead talked about other things. Family, hers, as mine was only my mum and she is dead, she told me about her parents, about her childhood, her teens, Daniel, being a mom, how proud of him she was. How he was cautious to tell her how much he loved politics but how she knew he loved it and was so happy that he had that side of his father and not the other.

We didn't dignify her ex-husband with a name. He didn't deserve any acknowledgment in my opinion. But Katherine wanted to talk about him, wanted to share her pain and I was more than happy to listen. If anything, it gave me the fire I needed to tell me that I wasn't keeping her alive just for sex, but I was keeping her alive for a very good reason.

He was a piece of work, there was no denying it. Katherine, after threatening a public separation if he didn't grant her a quiet divorce, had gone on to build her own wealth, her own life, and detach herself from him in every way possible. But he had risen through the political drought and she had watched in horror as the party rewarded him with promotion after promotion. He had charm, he had aged well, a good education, a polite manner, a kind face.

She kept quiet through fear but decided enough was enough when he was voted head of the Conservative Party, and with the general election set in just a few months, becoming Prime Minister was well within his reach, and she just couldn't bear to see a man like that running a country, never mind her own county, a country she loved.

I was indifferent to Great Britain. I neither liked nor disliked it. The country itself seemed to be fairer than many others, but it did have an odd selection of food choices and British people drank far too much tea.

I had a bad day...Have a cup of tea.

My dog died...Have a cup of tea.

I got a promotion!...Have a cup of tea.

My girlfriend left me...Have a cup of tea.

I won the lottery...Have a cup of tea.

I am going on the run from my ex-husband who is trying to have me murdered... Have a cup of tea.

It was like this magical beverage could be the right answer in any situation. For me, there could only ever be vodka.

One thing about Britain is it's posh women. I do love a posh British accent, and Katherine's, of course, was the finest. Although, (and perhaps because of the fact) I am feral, I always am attracted to class, elegance and grace in women.

Katherine had been to France a few times but as a traditional tourist only seeing the South of France in the summer and Paris once or twice for work or fancy weekends. Showing her this side of beautiful France was a pleasure for me. Getting her to taste the local delicacies, meet real French people, see the beautiful history of the villages, and get lost in its breath-taking countryside.

She opened to me sexually too, and I to her. Usually sexually, I would be dominant, demanding pleasure, leading the other person. But with Katherine, it felt like I was teaching her with care, guiding her, growing her confidence...and it awakened something inside of me too. It awakened a feeling I didn't know I had. It was indescribable, like her pleasure was all I could think of, and even when she was touching me, pleasing me, taking me higher, just seeing how much she enjoyed it too took me further than I had ever known possible.

My world exploded in all-new colors. I saw life differently. And whilst I didn't regret my past, I'm confident the people I killed deserved to die, it was true that that door was now closed for me. I couldn't imagine, even if all of this was resolved to an amicable outcome, that I would go back to killing in line with messages that were sent to me. I wanted more from my life. I wanted to cycle along French rivers and kiss beautiful women as the radio blared in rusty old fiats. I wanted to feel love and really live in a way that I hadn't yet. This time with Katherine had brought me to a place of change. I realised I didn't just want to keep her alive, I wanted to be with her properly and that was something I had never felt before.

I just had to make sure both of us survived, and first, we had to get this hike out of the way.

## 10

"Rabinovich?"

"Yes," he answered as he checked into the Fleur Èpanouie Hotel. The price tag was ridiculous but that was what fancy hotels did, had fancy names like Blooming Flowers and charged ridiculous prices that only idiots would pay, and Elena was used to a job expense account, and Katherine Scott-Webb was used to the finer things in life. For Rabinovich, he was happy with a hostel as long as he didn't have to share a bathroom with women. Their hair really did get everywhere and they took *forever.*

"Have you found them?" the voice asked with forced patience.

"No," Rabinovich answered with cold detachment as he walked around the suite that was home to Katherine and El just two nights before. He didn't expect to find anything obvious. The staff did a good job of house cleaning and Elena was a professional; she wasn't about to leave a map out with their direct route. But there were always clues.

"Nothing in her apartment?" At this Rabinovich rolled his eyes, he had known the address would be a dead end and a complete waste of his time. No way would Elena return to her home address, the Paris apartment when on the run, but his time was billed so he went where he was told and dutifully confirmed the suspicion. "She hasn't been there in a couple of weeks, not since the Mafia hit."

"How do you know ... Never mind."

He knew because who else would kill like that, he felt the distaste in his mouth as he recalled the crime scene photos. Body, cocaine, blood. Mess. They should have hired him. Although he knew she had gone in and out through a window. It was the only way the 'mystery' murder could have been committed. The window ledge walk had been impressive, he had to admit—36 floors up was nothing to turn your nose at. Rabinovich looked down at his widening gut. Too much bad food at greasy joints was not helping his waist-line, that was for sure, he really needed to get on top of it, but who needed to be super in shape when you could kill in over 200 ways without your victim even setting eyes on you. The motivation just wasn't there.

"So, where are they?" As Rabinovich paced around the hotel room he noticed something on the floor out of the corner of his eye. Dropping to his knees, his fingers ran through the thick hotel carpet. His nails trailing through the thick pile, collecting the mass, and after only a few seconds he pulled them up to his nose and took a deep breath.

One or two would be understandable, but this many...they had been here. That was the thing with women—their hair got everywhere.

"I know where they were, now I just need to track where they have gone."

"Call me when it is done and we are running out of time, Rabinovich. I need this sorted soon." The line clicked off and Rabinovich looked at his fingers in distaste. Everywhere.

~

THE HIKE WAS QUICKER than I expected. Katherine, when in the proper shoes, with a mapped-out route and in the know when it came to length and duration, could keep a pretty good pace. That and I had kept her worked out and in peak physical condition for the past few days.

I swear the air seemed to change as we reached closer to the chateau, like I could smell home in the air. I knew Kit would be able to smell our scent on the wind soon and he would be driving Aveline crazy trying to get her to let him out of the gate.

Those two were what made home home, and for the first time, I felt a panic. Bringing Katherine here, to Kit and Aveline, was a huge risk. I was putting their lives in danger for a stranger and that burden lay heavy on my shoulders. I was mixing home with work, opening my safe space, and now I had to do all I could to ensure that the chateau, if we were traced there, would keep us safe.

As we made our way across the final field, I took us down the dip and into the back ditch. The whole area is walled and topped with security fencing with only two entry points. The front gate and the back ditch; I don't just have a code but a thumb scan at this entrance and exit station. This is meant to be the secret entrance so if someone comes here looking, I want to know who and why.

I let us both in and Katherine wiped the sweat and dirt from her forehead. I could see the aches, she was tired, and to be honest, so was I.

"This place looks amazing," she said. And it did. Every time I came home, I was amazed by it. Then I heard the pounding of paws and a howl as Kit followed by Aveline came running across the lawn.

"KITTTTTT!" she hollered at the top of her voice. I don't think Aveline even knew about this entrance so I had no doubt she was in full-blown panic mode. Kit came bounding through the shrubbery and nearly knocked me straight off my feet, smothering and covering me in licks and kisses.

"Oh, my baby, you are such a good boy. Mwah mwah mwah. Who is mummy's good boy? Who is mummy's bestest boy? Give me all those kisses." I dropped down to him and wrapped him up in my arms as I gave him a ton of love and affection. I heard Katherine move a little behind me. Kit, whilst he had known she was there the whole time, took that moment to survey her.

It was a delicate moment; I think that Katherine could sense that Kit's approval would be important to me, so she stood still and let him judge her. He stepped closer, sniffy nose trailing over her feet, up her calves, nudging against her thigh as if to ask a question. The pause came and I held my breath, his tail perfectly still before he offered her bare knee one long lick.

At the sign of his approval, Katherine lowered slowly and gave Kit a soft stroke and a pat on his head. I knew that it wasn't his favorite but he let her anyway, which spoke volumes to me, and just as we were all having a bonding moment, Aveline burst through the bushes.

Her squeal set us all on edge as it echoed through the gardens and off across the fields.

"For goodness sake, Elena!" she exclaimed after a long list of expletives in French. "Can't you ever call and tell me you are on your way home!? And why are you in the garden? And why didn't you tell me you were bringing a guest- I would have made up a room," She turned and headed back towards the house still muttering under her breath.

"Erm. You didn't tell me you were... married," Katherine said in a half joke, half serious reply.

"Yes, it would seem so on the outside as though I was, but no, Aveline is actually the dog walker."

Even though Aveline is a few yards in front she turned on one heel with a mock scowl. "The dog walker!" she blustered. "I keep this house in perfect condition, I lovingly tend to your dog whilst you have your crazy schedule, I cook, I clean, and the dog doesn't even need walking, he walks himself!" she exclaimed.

I smiled at her frown and bounded over, wrapping my arms around her in a tight bear hug. "You know that Kit and I wouldn't be here without you so stop frowning and tell me what deliciousness you are cooking up. This is Katherine, by the way, she is staying around for a while, she will stay in my room with me."

Aveline flushed at my display of warmth or possibly at my abrupt coming out- I've never brought women home before- and then turned to Katherine. "I apologize for my rudeness, just El always manages to get me flustered. Welcome to the chateau, Katherine. It is a beautiful name, I think that ..."

Katherine walked alongside Aveline and listened as she began to chatter away. I watched them as my fingers curled through Kit's thick fur. "We are going to have to really work these next few weeks, Kit. We have to keep them safe, okay?"

And I swear he nodded.

## 11

"Rabinovich?"

"Yes." He held back on the sigh because to be fair to his employer he had been given two days to get on with his job, unfortunately, he still needed a little longer.

He had tracked Elena and Katherine Scott-Webb on the next legs of their great getaway. It had involved all kinds of inventive ways of travel. Elena would have known it was futile in the long run, but she had bought the pair time. Now Rabinovich was within sniffing distance. He had found the last car they had ditched and he had to presume they were now on foot.

*Elena has a lair round here. I can practically smell it.*

Rabinovich was currently in the local bibliothèque speaking in hushed tones as he cross-referenced the local land map with recent purchases. He knew the exact start of Elena and Katherine Scott-Webb's hike and the rough distance they could cover before dark. Drawing a time circle from the point of origin gave him 11 properties that they could now be in. Some were easy to rule out, but realistically he was left with three options. Three possibilities of where they could be hiding out.

Now he just had to track them down.

"Update?"

"Three properties. They are in one of them. Once I have found which, it will only be a matter of time." He kept his voice low as he flicked through the house deeds for each of the three properties. Assessing the layouts, the weak spots, points of entry.

"Good. I need clean, Rabinovich."

"Noted. And Elena? Alive or not?" It was his employer's turn to let out a deep sigh. Rabinovich could hear the wheels turning as he clicked his tongue.

"Bring her in if possible. I don't know what the fuck she is up to. She needs bringing back in line. It would be a shame to lose an operative of her calibre but she has been more and more rogue lately. If she won't come in, then do what you must."

"Understood." The line clicked and the call ended. Rabinovich poured over the floor plans and made some mental notes about access points, vantage places he could make observations unseen.

*Oh, Elena, the net is closing and you have no idea.*

"When? Okay. No ... Yes. Thank you." I hung up the phone and noted that I needed to remember to make a larger donation to the local library. I started to pace, my mind whizzing into overdrive. That was the thing with the old school operatives. They were cautious of Google, of the tracking, the check-ins, the search history... they would always go traditional routes where they could, but luckily local librarians have always had a keen eye and a nose for gossip.

Julia had spotted Rabinovich the second he had entered with his Russian accent and less-than-approachable demeanor and she had done exactly as I had previously instructed: removed my house plans from the public records and notified me the moment he had left.

I thought that I had bought Katherine a few more days than we had. We had only been in the chateau less than a week and to give her credit, every day she had sat down and continued to write her book. I watched her power through the hard pages. I watched the memories surface and I kissed her cheeks when tears spilled down them, but she typed through, a woman on a mission to finish, and she was nearing the end. But she needed a little more time, and that meant I needed to take care of Rabinovich once and for all.

It was inevitable he would find us eventually.

He had a job to do and so did I. My diversion had bought me two days, more or less, and in that time a decision had to be made, hunt or be hunted. Rabinovich would be stalking the three other viable possibilities. I could try and get to him while he was searching and assessing them.

Or, I could wait for him to realize we were somewhere else, it would be easy for him to find us from that point. A drive around, a drone, even a few well-placed questions would lead him straight up to our front drive.

I would have the advantage. I knew this place like the back of my hand, I could see it too through his eyes. I knew the logical points at which to gain entry. I could set my traps, bait him, and then take him out. The problem with this plan was Aveline. Kit. Katherine. There was a high price of collateral if I made a mistake.

But, then again. I didn't make mistakes.

I had so much to protect. I thought for a second of my mother and me being her liability and ultimately her downfall and I screwed my face up thinking of all the liabilities I was building up. This was not a game for the faint hearted.

So, I would wait for Rabinovich. I would set the scene; I would stack the deck and I would wait to be hunted. I could be prey for a day, pretend I didn't know he was coming, and then at the right moment, I would flip the table. For all my annoyance at Rabinovich, I didn't relish taking him out. I had a respect for him, and my mother wouldn't approve of taking out an assassin unless it was absolutely necessary, it was the hitman's code to respect one another.

But, what it was all coming down to was Katherine or Rabinovich, and I knew I had already made my choice.

I headed through the house to the kitchen where Aveline was singing along to the radio under her breath as she prepared pastries for dessert. Her hands worked methodically with a pace even I could envy; she cooked with such love, care and passion.

"Aveline, I need to talk to you about something." She paused her knife that hovered over the ripe green apples. Cinnamon and vanilla filled the air, and my stomach rumbled.

"Okay. Tell me," she replied and turned, rolling up her sleeves and preparing herself.

"A time may come in the next few days where I tell you to do something. That might be to call a number, take the car, go down into the basement, hide. Run. I don't want to panic you, but at the same time, it is very *very* important that you do exactly as I ask, okay? I know that may seem unfair that I don't tell you everything, but it is really important that you do exactly as I say."

Aveline paused, setting her knife on the side. "I have never asked what you do, El. I have never questioned what takes you away in the middle of the night. Why you practice shooting across the lawn, why you have knives and guns hidden in random places, how you live such a wealthy lifestyle, and yet your job is sporadic at best. I don't ask, because ..." She looked up at me with her big, warm, hazel eyes, "I don't ask because you saved me. You gave me a home. A purpose. A life. And all you have ever really asked in return is... don't ask questions. So, if you tell me tomorrow to run, I will run. If you tell me the day after to hide, I will hide. And if you tell me that I need to get Kit and Katherine and drive as far away from here as possible, I will do it. Okay?" Her French feistiness flared in each word and I marveled at the strong beautiful woman she had become.

I felt emotions bubble below my icy exterior, a lump in my throat formed, and with all the effort I could muster, I gave Aveline a nod and a weak smile. She nodded in return and turned back to her pastries. "Does Katherine like apple because I didn't ask and now I already started."

I smiled to myself.

"I will go and ask her."

I made my way upstairs to find Katherine in her usual spot in the bay window, leaning against the lead panes, overlooking the rolling French countryside that spans out as far as the eye can see. "How is it coming along?" I asked softly as I dropped a kiss on her forehead. She let out a tiny sigh.

"Maybe a chapter or two left. It would help if I could send it to Daniel, do you think that is possible? I would like to get his opinion, he helped me a lot before. Do you think it is possible? I hate to cause you any more issues."

I ran through the options; they knew

now she was alive. I could reroute the email with no issue. It would probably be a good idea to have a copy out in the open anyway, just in case. "Just mail it. Is that all you need?" I asked.

Katherine pulled a face.

"Well, it would be better if I could mail it and then speak to him afterwards. So he can give me his opinion, let me know if it is okay. I know he isn't a publisher or anything. But...Well, he is my son and it will directly affect him. Can you do that?"

"For you, I can do anything," I whispered as I continued to bend lower, peppering her cheeks with soft airy kisses and I wondered at the wisdom of my words.

"Write the email and I will send it now, tell him in it you will call in a few hours so he will expect a call from an unknown number, okay? But don't give him any more details than that; I don't want to put a target on his back."

I could hear her breath quicken, feel her pulse speed up and her cheeks flush as my kisses continued. She murmured her agreement and I slowly pulled away. "Good, then come to the bathroom." I sauntered out of the room, feeling her eyes on me before pausing at the doorframe where I turned and asked, "Also, do you like apple pastries?"

She looked back at me quizzically, then raised her eyebrows with a what-is-normal-anymore questioning glance. "Yes, I like apple."

I LET the tub fill to the top. The bathroom has been one of my favorite places to design and watch come alive. There were plenty of bathrooms in total in the chateau, but this one...this one was mine. I had a perfectly good bathroom next to my bedroom. This one was on the very top floor of five floors. In this one there was nothing except a large, oversized tub that sat on cast iron feet. I had had huge skylight windows put in when I had the old leaking roof of the chateau replaced, so in this bathroom, you could lie back in the tub and feel the sun beaming in through the huge windows or enjoy a drink looking out and up at the stars.

The water was hot and filled with luxurious scents and bubbles I had bought in some Parisian boutique a few months ago. I lit some candles I had found in a kitchen cabinet.

*Who even am I?*

Katherine walked in in a robe which she dropped and walked towards the tub. Her nude body was beautiful and every time I saw it I admired her. I would tell her she was beautiful and she would become bashful and shy and point out all the parts she didn't find beautiful in herself and ask me how could I possibly find her body beautiful when mine was perfect.

My body is lean and hard where it needs to be. My body is a weapon I have carefully crafted over years to keep me safe in the work I do.

Katherine's body is soft, delicate and feminine. The silvery lines she hates on her belly and breasts from her pregnancy, I find lovely. I like to draw along them with my tongue. The ass and thighs she fears are too big, are gorgeous, round and a place I love to explore. Katherine's body has been built for others over the years- a body to be looked at and critiqued by her husband and the general public, a body to grow a child, a body supposed to become perfect again after pregnancy. No wonder Katherine worries what people think of her body.

My body has never been judged by those parameters so I cannot imagine what that feels like.

I judge my own body by how much it can lift and how fast it can move. I can make it look certain ways in certain clothes in a mirror to fit whichever job I need it to, but other than that, it doesn't matter to me what it looks like. My body can be masculine, feminine or anything in between.

All I can do is love her body, every part of it. Every time I see it, I love it more.

She slid into the warm water, her skin is pale, blushes easily, it is so very *English*.

She is slightly taller than me, but it is never something I'm conscious of. Her feet reached the end of the tub and she was effortlessly lovely.

The steam rose in soft swirls and water splashed lightly over the side every time she moved.

Katherine lay back, her skin turning pink in the rising steam. Already her cheeks were flushed. The tips of her long chocolate brown hair were wet as they brushed the bubbles and dipped into the hot soapy water.

"I feel shy," she said softly, and my heart melted.

"You don't ever need to feel shy with me," I replied as I lowered myself down into the hot water. I love it when the bath is so hot it takes your breath for a second. That you can feel the sting as the burn hovers. The flash of pleasure between pain, sensually caressing every inch of your skin; divine.

"I know you think my body is beautiful, but, I just don't have the same confidence you do. This is a big deal for me, right here. Knowing you are looking at me."

I nodded. "Katherine, for so many years your body has been judged by others. Your mindset and insecurities won't just change overnight. My body has never been offered up for others to judge. So I don't think of it like that. None of us are perfect, but that doesn't mean we cannot be beautiful. So, for now, let me just love your body for you? How about that?

I leant forwards and I touched her hair, tenderly. I pushed it back behind her ear so I could see her face.

"There's another thing." Katherine's eyes met mine for a second before they looked down at her thighs in the water. "I know, well sexually, I mean, well for me, our sex, it has been amazing. Just incredible. Life changing. I had never known sex could be like that. Just, I know I haven't, well, made love to you, yet. It's just... I mean, I want to, so very badly. I think about it a lot. I just... I'm just...I don't have the experience. I don't know how to please a woman. I'm not sure I ever knew how to please men either. Not really. I'm worried I will be terrible at it."

My hand slid beneath the bubbles and my fingers reached for hers, entwining, threading, giving her a soft, reassuring squeeze. "Would you like me to show you?" I asked gently. She paused for a moment, and then nodded slowly with a gentle bite of nerves to her lip for good measure.

I brought her palms towards me,

guiding her hands up my inner thighs. She glided effortlessly over my skin, soft palms on creamy thighs. I slid down the tub a little, raising both legs out and then hooking my knees over the lip so I half lay, half sat, spread out for her.

My fingers loosened and then settled at her wrist as her fingertips hovered against the puffy lips of my sex. "First, you have to tease; hint at what you're going to do, how you are going to touch me. Like this." I guided her fingers down so they stroked lightly against my smooth lips. I had shaved earlier and they felt baby soft and I liked it. I felt myself responding, aching already for more, for her fingers to move just an inch to the right. "Then you might touch me, just to keep me on edge for you." I moved her hand in and let her fingers trail through my flushed sex. I gasped a little at her sweet, inexperienced touch—if only she knew what she did to me.

"Now, think about your own body. What would you like now, how do you touch yourself? Do that to me. Soft." I made her touch lightly. "Hard." I made her fingers press hard against my sex. "Slow." I twisted her palm and her fingers circled a little around my clit. "Fast." I directed her hand faster and the tips of her fingers swirled quicker and quicker around my aching bud until my thighs trembled and I felt my own pulse racing throughout my body.

"You see. You can just play, if you want, try different things. I like penetration, you can put your fingers inside me and your thumb against my clit if you like? Watch me, watch my response to everything you'll soon know what I like the most." I gasped as my hand fell away, offering myself to her, giving her back the control. Her fingers stilled, her eyes on me, staring intensely, measuring my reactions, watching how I respond. She continued, taking over with confidence that rose up slowly. She moved closer, sliding between my parted thighs. Her breasts rose out of the water, covered in iridescent soapy bubbles, and as her thumb swept up and over my clit, my body bucked, and water splashed in waves over the lip of the tub spraying across the floor.

She got closer, closer. Her hand between our bodies as our breasts touched and then I felt her lips on my skin and her hand teasing and then her fingers pushing inside me. I was so turned on by the fact of it being her, it suddenly didn't matter how good or bad it was. She kissed along my collarbone as I thrust lightly against her fingers, opening myself up to her, giving her my body to have, explore and enjoy.

I gave in to the pleasure. I didn't ride it out or try to make it last. She was what I had wanted for days, or perhaps even unknowingly, for years. I let myself enjoy the shudderingly hard waves of my climax. Her hand stilled and her palm pressed flat so she could give me the pressure I want to enjoy against her. Her lips inched closer and closer to mine until they stole my moans away with deep lingering kisses.

She took my hand once more and brought my fingers between her thighs. She looked at me with those eyes that I knew I couldn't resist and my hand slid between her thighs.

*Katherine, what are you doing to me?*

## 12

"Rabinovich?"

"Yes?" He sighed deeply. It had only been a few hours; he had been to two of the properties and they were both dead ends. It had to be this last place or it was back to the drawing board but pausing his surveillance to answer the phone was getting tiresome.

"Did you fucking find them?! Katherine Scott-Webb needs to be found! And she needs to be silenced. Jesus fucking Christ. An ex-wife causing more problems than I have known a president to cause." Rabinovich waited calmly for the voice to stop ranting before he replied.

"It will be done when it is done. I am closing in."

"Just make sure it *is* done, Rabinovich, because I don't want to be hiring someone else to sort all this mess out once and for all." The line clicked off before Rabinovich could reply. *Fucking asshole*, he thought, clicking the eyepiece back into place so he could peer through an empty darkened window.

"Oh, Daniel, it is *so* good to hear your voice. I hated leaving you to worry, but I had to get out of London." Katherine held the phone out in front of her on a loudspeaker, wrapped in a fluffy white dressing gown, her hair was still wet from the tub.

I didn't want to listen in on their conversation. I wanted them to have time to talk without me hovering, but I needed to listen for the click on the line, the threat, maybe Daniel wasn't alone. All these things were important not only for his safety but for Katherine's also.

"I have never been so pleased to get an

encrypted email," Daniel replied with a hint of a smile that I could picture on his handsome face. But I could tell he had been worried, he hadn't had much sleep, and anxiety vibrated through his words. "Are you sure you're safe? That it is okay to call?"

I moved to slip out of the room and give them some privacy. Daniel was not in any immediate threat and the call from our side was untraceable. I felt okay letting her be a mom and reassuring her only son that although his mother was on the run with an assassin on her trail, sent by his father, she was, in fact, okay and safe.

"Yes, Daniel, it is okay. The call can't be traced," Katherine replied.

"You don't understand, Mum, I have to tell you something. Someone is after you. They came up here. I saw them. It was probably whoever has been sent by dad. I knew something was off with them, but I let my own ego...well, never mind. The point is that it didn't sit right with me. I checked and they never even sent anyone to interview me for an internship. And then you disappeared. There was no sign of a break-in at your place, but it was weird."

I could go in now and cut the call, but it would raise more questions.

"Yes, Daniel, I know that, I know someone is trying to kill me. That is why I had to leave; your father sent someone so that I didn't finish the book. If anything happens you have a copy now, you can at least... Well, at least people will know the truth."

I heard Katherine's voice break a little, anxiety mixed with panic and worry. I wanted to hold her, wrap her up and tell her all would be okay. I felt so torn, wondering what to do for the best and then...

" I just can't believe this is happening; it doesn't seem real and as for Dad...I just can't, I mean, I know who he is, I know what he did to you, but that was the heat-of-the-moment rage. This...it's cold, calculated. I just.... Fuck, I hate him."

I heard the shift in Katherine's voice, the mother instinct kicking in. "Your father can only see one outcome now; he is desperate to be Prime Minister. It clouds his judgment, takes over his every thought

and I am a threat to that. He will do anything to stop my book from being
published."

"I know. Mum, just stay safe. Please."

"I am trying my best, sweetheart."

She smiled and I felt my heart lift as I
moved away to give them some space.

I meandered a little through the
chateau. I loved my home before, but now
with Katherine, it felt different. It didn't feel
so big and empty.

Life, warmth, and laughter echoed
through the hallways. Aveline and Kit were
still here, happy, with their own space, but
Katherine seeped into the corners, all the
nooks and crannies. Like she was a force
that I had no control over. She touched my
life in so many ways and gave me a
purpose.

I made my way back to the study; I
couldn't hear Katherine speaking anymore
so I assumed the conversation had finished.
I entered slowly, peering around the edge
of the door, but Katherine was looking out
of the window over and across the rolling
hills of the French countryside. The flowers
of Aveline's garden were bursting in color,

though it was still a little cold, all from her love and affection.

I stepped up behind her, wrapping my arms around her waist and pulling her back against me. "It is going to be okay, Katherine. Daniel is safe, and as long as you are here, I can protect you. Everything is going to go back to normal soon, I promise. You will see him again in no time."

I could tell something was wrong, she was stiff in my arms, refusing to relax into my embrace. Holding onto a wave of anger, a pain. "Katherine," I murmured, nuzzling in against her neck, "It is going to be okay."

"Is it?" She pulled herself from my arms and turned to face me. "Is it going to be okay, El?" Her words were laced with pain, hurt, anger.

"Yes," I replied with a burrowing of my eyebrows. "Are you okay? Is Daniel okay?"

Katherine laughed ironically.

"Yes, Daniel is fine, worried. So worried, but safe. He wouldn't be quite so worried except he had a visit recently. From a woman pretending to offer him an internship. Except it turns out she was much more interested in the book I was writing.

She poked and prodded about that and then disappeared."

Ah.

"Except she didn't disappear, did she, El? She got on a train and came to my home, and then she broke into my house and told me that I was in great danger." She began to wave her hands, insinuating how grave the situation was. "That woman, with no name, was sent to kill me. Am I right? Daniel sent a clip from the cafe CCTV where you met him. You might have been disguised but I would recognise you anywhere. " Katherine laughed shrilly to herself. She held up the phone with a shaking hand, her fingers white and trembling and she showed me.

The image was a still from the café shop's internal CCTV, it was grainy and distorted but there was no denying it, even in my disguise that I thought was so perfect, it most definitely was me. It was absolutely me.

"Katherine. Please. I can explain," I started to reply, moving to her, to touch her, but she shook me off.

"I don't want you to explain. I want an

answer. A really simple answer. You have been lying to me." I could feel the bile rise in my throat. A panic setting in already. I knew what she would ask, and I knew that I could not lie to her. But also, the truth. Well, the truth would end us. Of course it would. Her voice dropped to barely a whisper, the anger evaporating as she asked with almost a plea. Hoping, desperate that her instincts were wrong and that it wasn't true.

"Were you going to kill me, El?"

I let my hand fall away and I took a step back, my eyes fell closed and I composed myself. I knew it would happen one day. I just thought maybe we would have more time before she would see the monster I truly was. That maybe she would have had the time to see the good in me too, to see that that part of me, is not all I am.

"From the moment I saw you, watched you, knew you, there was no doubt in my mind. I could not kill you, but I don't think that is the question you are asking me. I'll do anything to protect you. You know I will."

She began to cry, her eyes filled slowly,

and I could count the seconds between each blink, watch as the droplets fell and skimmed her cheeks. I am a messy crier, ugly, runny nose, sniffles, can't catch my breath. Katherine cries with beauty like she is barely aware of what is happening. That she can't stop herself even if she wanted to, just natural emotional responses.

She looked up at me, her eyes filled with tears, "Do you kill people, is that what you do? Your job?"

I nodded slowly and I couldn't meet her eyes, suddenly ashamed of a career I had spent a lifetime perfecting.

"Were you sent to kill me?"

I didn't need to answer, she already knew, but the masochistic side to her needed the proof, the validation. So I nodded, no longer able to form words.

"I thought you were different, but you are just the same really. A monster. Just a different type."

And with that, she brushed past me and headed down the stairs.

$\sim$

KATHERINE KNEW she was in mortal danger and though she didn't want to be anywhere near me, she also seemed to know that I was her best hope. She spent her time in the kitchen with Aveline mainly editing and finishing her book. She barely spoke and when she did it was only in response to Aveline's questions about food. I listened, I waited, hoping for her forgiveness, but I knew in my heart it wouldn't come.

The tap-tapping of her nails against the keys was the only comfort I could find. Kit seemed to sense my pain and hovered around me more than normal, looking for ways in which he could comfort me, but unfortunately, he cannot fix what I am, the things I have done, the darkness inside of me.

Katherine has been hurt too many times in the past, she has a strength that now allows her to cut through the pain and to make the hard choice. No matter what it was she felt for me, there is no doubt in my mind that she no longer felt it.

I threw myself into work, and by that, I mean I waited patiently to be hunted.

## 13

---

"Rabinovich?"

"Yes?" Rabinovich couldn't keep the hint of a smile out of his voice. After two days of a wild goose chase, he had finally conceded the fact that Elena had outsmarted him. Once. He had learned from his mistake and decided to embrace modern technology, not bother asking people—they were all liars anyway—and set up a drone.

After checking out the coverage for an hour or so, he had found a property that was not listed in the library and he knew it was hers. To be thorough he had done his homework and due diligence and confirmed without a doubt that Elena owned the property and now he lay in the tall grass about a mile out to the west with binoculars he had just confirmed a sighting of Katherine Scott-Webb in the upper left bathroom. She looked sad, her fingers had lingered over the lip of the tub as she seemed to stare out straight at him, but of course, she had no idea he was there. Hiding. Watching her.

If he had brought his rifle, she would be dead before those pretty pink nails left the rim of the bath, but he hadn't expected Elena to leave her so exposed. So easily sighted, plus this was only supposed to be a confirmation. The fun part was about to start.

"Have you found them, Rabinovich?"

"Yes," Rabinovitch replied with a curling sneer as he saw Elena herself come into view and usher Katherine away from the window. "Twenty-four hours and the job will be done."

"Good. Clean. No mistakes."

∾

I ASKED Katherine to stand at the window. I hated that it had to be here, in this bathroom, but it offered the best view. Rabinovich's drone had triggered my sensors a few hours before and I knew the route he would take by foot. The tall grass offered him the perfect coverage; he could observe undetected until he had proof of life. I had to give him that. If he didn't see Katherine alive and well, he would be more cautious. He would want to take the long shot then hunt me down after. I needed him to feel confident enough to enter the property for a close kill in which he could then take me at the same time. To give him that confidence I had to appear unaware, cocky, sloppy.

This is why Katherine stood trembling at the window, in the place she least wanted to be in the entire house. With me in the same vicinity, it seemed to make her skin crawl and she nervously held herself.

I had no doubt that was the plan. I was a liability but not a lost cause. Maybe a few months in the hole would realign my views with my employer. Perhaps then I would not go off book and start rescuing the people I was supposed to be killing. Well, he would hope that because, after all, I was a good investment, but he was mistaken. The hole didn't bother me. It never had; my mother had taught me how to work through mental torture in an easy systematic way, and my views would not be realigned. Anyway, Rabinovich was not going to have the chance to bring me in because I was going to kill him first. It was the only way this would end.

I watched as he packed up his things, cut his call and made his way back out of the field. He would come later, just as dusk began to settle. It is what I would do; it would offer him the cover of darkness and the best element of surprise whilst still being able to get his bearings in the fading sun.

I looked at my clock. It gave us three hours and, of course, a feast to finish.

∿

"AVELINE," I said as I took a seat at the long dining table opposite Katherine but enough to the left a little so she could avoid eye contact with me if she wanted to, "We have 45 minutes and then we have to get moving, okay?"

There was a buzz in the air. Katherine knew Rabinovich was outside, Aveline knew something was about to happen and Kit could sense the tension. But Aveline had decided in her infinite wisdom that if all hell was about to break loose, it might as well happen when we all had full stomachs. She had really pushed the boat out and made a collection of dishes that made my mouth water. Even Katherine, who could barely think about food, couldn't help but let out a little moan as perfectly baked bread, drizzled in oil and brushed with balsamic, crushed between her teeth, and her tongue tasted the explosion of freshly picked tomatoes, diced onions, and melted smoked cheese.

"Katherine, you never said, how did you and El meet?" Aveline asked kindly with a warm smile, and I held back my daggers. Katherine hesitated and then answered with a hint of sarcasm.

"She was saving me from a mortal danger." I'm still not sure whether Aveline was playing cute or if the sarcasm was lost in translation, but she offered Katherine a warm smile.

"Oh, we have that in common then." I watched Katherine's fork still and her eyes rise, her interest piqued.

"She saved you?" she asked quietly, and I felt the need to clarify.

"No, I didn't save Aveline. I just—"

"Excuse me," Aveline cut through with mock abrasion. "I think that I will be the one to tell this story." I sat back in my chair holding my hands up in apology and Aveline began to talk.

"El may not think she saved me as I wasn't dying in the street. I hadn't been hit by a car, I wasn't choking on food or drowning in the lake. But I think my actual reality was a lot worse. Those kinds of pains...they come once and you either heal or you die, but either way, it is over. My pain was never-ending. A hole of constant hurt that came again and again from the people who were supposed to love me the most. I was drowning, I was choking, I was dying just this slow and painful death. El... she didn't need to save me. She could have walked right by like every other person did. The ones who knew what was happening but said nothing, that did nothing...But she didn't. She gave me an escape, and even when I was terrified to take it, scared of my own shadow, she held my hand and showed me that I deserved to be in the sun."

Aveline paused, reaching forwards to take a drink of her ruby red French wine. "Some people may not understand now why I choose to live here, in this house alone a lot, while El is away, with just Kit to keep my company. But I do it because I feel safe and El never pushes me. She lets me do things at my own time and pace, whilst offering me this beautiful home to live in and share. I feel very lucky."

A lump rose in my throat. She drove me crazy, this girl, but she had come so far, done so well—I am so proud of her. Maybe I should tell her that more, but it isn't really my way and as if she read my thoughts, she continued.

"It isn't really our way to say these things. And I don't think we need to, I just think maybe when it seems like we are on

the brink of some big change, it is important to remember who we are and what
brought us together. It gives us a reason,
you know?"

I nodded and lifted my glass of water; a
light tilt of my glass and we drank together.
Katherine watched us both, and I could see
that she was torn. Perhaps she saw herself
reflected in Aveline's words but her own
morals and ethics wouldn't let her step over
the hurdle of my occupation. The thing I
do that pays for this house, this food, this
lifestyle.

"You are both lucky to have found each
other," Katherine said gently as she too
took a drink of her wine. I watched her fingers curl around the slim stem, the same
way they did the very first time I saw her in
her apartment. She glanced over at me and
our gazes lingered for a moment or two.

I felt the pain rise in me, the loss of our
connection. The end of our relationship
and what it could have been. I knew how
she made me feel, the way life sparkled
with her, how I could see the best in myself
and finally a clear way forwards on how to
leave this life and lifestyle behind once and

for all. Move on to a good, healthy, normal, functioning life filled with happiness, joy, maybe even love.

"Didn't you say we only had forty-five minutes?" asked Aveline, and I dragged my gaze away from Katherine to check the clock. She was right.

It was time.

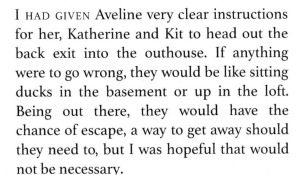

I HAD GIVEN Aveline very clear instructions for her, Katherine and Kit to head out the back exit into the outhouse. If anything were to go wrong, they would be like sitting ducks in the basement or up in the loft. Being out there, they would have the chance of escape, a way to get away should they need to, but I was hopeful that would not be necessary.

Aveline had never held a gun before and I don't think Katherine had ever seen one in real life, but I gave them both one anyway. They would probably be more in danger of themselves and each other than Rabinovich, but I didn't want to leave them without any defense.

I left the house looking unprotected and lived in as I made my way outside. The left side dining room window had been left open, and I knew Rabinovich would take that as his point of entry. I was dressed head to toe in black, tight Nike Lycra, my hair was pulled back tight. I had stretched and I felt lithe, the adrenaline surging as I cracked my neck, hands, fingers, and toes.

I slinked off to the right-side ditch and took my position, lying flat to the ground, eyepiece in place and night vision on. I had the heat sensor activated too so when the darkness finally settled, I would be able to detect Rabinovich before he even knew I pulled the trigger.

I waited in complete silence, even my breaths couldn't be heard, I was perfectly still in wait. My eyes flickered from the lenses to the sensors. Nothing triggered, no heat—yet, but it wouldn't be long. Rabinovich would be at the top of his game.

It was strange, but I knew he was there before any of the high-tech equipment even picked him up. Maybe because I thought like him, I could already see what he would do before he did it, so I was just waiting in expectation as he cut across the front lawn and slipped down the side of the building.

My finger stroked the trigger...any second now...

## 14

Rabinovich caught the open window and made his way across the front of the house and slipped down the side. He was about to make his way back to the window when something stopped him. It was all too easy. El may not know that he was here, but she would know that he was at least in the vicinity from that stupid librarian bitch. She was many things, but she was not sloppy. He dipped down and at that precise second, a bullet cracked past the side of his head.

He didn't have time to react before the next one came and clipped his shoulder.

"Fuck!" he exclaimed and slunk around the side of the house and out of the shooter's line.

He was furious that she had outsmarted him and lured him into her trap, but he also felt a smugness, because now her one big advantage was gone. He knew where she was, he knew what her weapon was, and he wasn't dead. He slipped his belt from the loops and wrapped it tight around his arm. The bullet had only nicked him, but the blood was pouring in a steady stream and he didn't want to feel the slightest bit light-headed. She was too good with a rifle for that. He ripped the leather with his teeth, making the belt pull tight and hard around his bicep, and figured out his new plan.

～

"Fuck!" I hissed under my breath. He moved at the last second and the first shot missed him completely. The second was a last-ditch attempt as he now knew where I was, but it only nicked him, nothing more. I lay flat to the ground and ran through my options; I couldn't believe it. It had been perfect. The perfect setup for the perfect kill. Maybe that had been the problem. I had been too clever, if there was such a thing.

Well, what was done was done. Now I had to readjust and adapt. I kicked the AK-74M rifle down the ditch, it was no use to me now. My hands reached to my ankles and I pulled the PSM pistol from its clip and flicked the safety, then I took the Gerber Mark II Fixed blade knife from my boot. I slid down the ditch a few feet or so and then made my way along the banking to rise up at the other side of Rabinovich. I had a tactical advantage but he had years of experience and he knew me.

I rose up the banking, knowing he had moved, hoping he had inched closer to where the bullet had fired from.

He hadn't.

I heard the click and dropped to my knees in a slow roll before the gun fired. My AK-74M had a silencer, his Glock did not, and the crack of the bullet echoed around the valley. But then I heard the howl from Kit coming from the outhouse.

Rabinovich grinned at me with a sly smile. "Oh, El. I thought you knew better."

The game changed. He didn't need to hunt me, he needed his mark, and I would follow. He spun off and ducked away, making his way to the sound of Kit's desperate howl.

I knew leaving Kit with them was a risk, but I also knew I couldn't have Kit loose in the grounds- Rabinovich would have shot him from a distance for sure. I cursed again and began my own pursuit, taking a long way around. I was faster and knew the grounds better.

We arrived at near enough the same time, the difference being that I had my gun on him there as he didn't know where I would be coming from. I fired three rounds; the first hit, the second planted in his shoulder, the third nicked the leather of his belt and buried into the muscle of his bicep.

He was a tough son of a bitch. He didn't even pause, but he began to fire back with reckless abandon. He shoulder-barged into the door as he kept me back with a hail of bullets, knowing I would be reluctant to fire in the direction of the outhouse. "Aveline," I shouted with a forced cold calm. "Do no open the door."

His gun began to click, he was out of bullets and I wasn't about to give him time to refill. With my Gerber Mark II Fixed blade knife gripped tight in my right hand, I cleared the lawn in seconds, with a launch from the ball of my foot I pounced. My legs wrapped around him as my hands gripped his skull. I felt the slow-spreading sting as his own knife sank into my outer thigh; he pressed with a hard force so the hilt rested at my skin.

He hadn't hit my artery but the blood poured down my leg, the adrenaline numbed the pain, endorphins kicked in allowing me to function. I took my own blade but he knocked it away with his forearm taking the brunt.

Rabinovich spun around and then fell back hard against the thick wooden door, trapping me in place, winding me with the force. He raised his arm up and I felt his elbow connect with my face, crashing into my jaw, nose, and lip. My entire body shunted back, my fingers reached for the bullet holes in his shoulder and arms and pressed hard into his exposed flesh. He let out a low roar as I scraped at his wounds, and I knew that he was losing a lot of blood. To try and stop the pain he stepped forward to shake me off, but I dropped easily, landing in a crouch.

My hands curled around the handle of his blade and I pulled it from my thigh. I didn't feel a thing as we circled each other. I had his knife and he didn't have a visible weapon, but that didn't mean he was unarmed. I heard the lock of the door click behind me, and I could have screamed. One thing. One fucking thing I asked. But I couldn't think about that now.

"Oh, come on, El, my orders are to bring you in, not kill you. Is it worth this? Do you want to die? You are happy to die for what? Some rich English bitch?" Rabinovich sneered. I cleared my throat, spitting the blood from my mouth as my eyes flashed wild and feral back at him.

"I am prepared to die for her. What are you dying for, Rabinovich?" I asked with a coldness; his eyebrows rose in surprise at my admission.

"You die for love? This is what you are fighting for? Some fanciful notion of love? Well, for me it is simple," he said with a low scoff, "I am not going to die. Not here. Not tonight. Not at the hands of a girl."

The door opened just an inch. I knew it had to be Katherine; Aveline would never disobey me. I caught her eye in the gap and I tried to give her a reassuring smile, but I knew it didn't reach my eyes. Katherine may have only opened the door an inch, but Kit had other ideas. He could smell my blood; he could sense my danger. And he had my enemy in his sights.

He jumped with full force and barreled out of the door, his teeth in a hard snarl as they sank into Rabinovitch's calf. They tore at his limb, sinking into his flesh again and again with rumbling growls as Kit gave all he could to buy his mistress some time, but it wasn't enough.

"NO !!!" I cried out as I watched Rabinovitch pull another blade from his waist. I closed my eyes, but I heard the whimpering cry as Kit fell heavy to the ground. As my eyes opened, I watched the blood spread, dying his fur a deep crimson red.

Rage.

It consumed me.

We moved at the same time. Cut from the same KGB cloth, his first hand knowledge, mine second. The difference though is that I knew what he would do. It was so ingrained into him he didn't even realize how predictable it was.

His hand reached for my knife-holding wrist, knowing he had the advantage of strength. So, I dropped his knife and caught it in my other. As he pinned me, I felt my right wrist break, snapping under the sheer force of his grip, and his left hand closed around my throat ready to squeeze the life out of me, to take my dying breath. Before he could anticipate my move, my left hand drove upwards piercing just beneath his ribs and driving upwards towards his heart.

Rabinovich's knife was sharpened to perfection. It cut through his flesh as though it were air. I saw his eyes bulge as the shock registered, and I turned the blade inside him. His hands didn't slacken, my lungs cried for air as he squeezed harder and harder. I could do no more. I felt his weight fall down on me, hot wet blood soaking through my clothes—his blood, not mine. It was just a case now of who would die first. If it was him, I would live; if it was me...Well, we would both die.

That was my last thought as the world went black.

## 15

I heard the beeps and whirls of machines. But the room faded in and out of focus. Bright white fluorescent lights merged with dreams. Reality and my subconscious thoughts became indistinguishable as I drifted between here and not here.

I was alive, that much I knew. I could feel the sting of fresh stiches in my thigh and the ache in my back where Rabinovitch slammed me against the door.

Everything flashed, each moment played over on repeat, always ending with the whimpering howl of Kit as he fell to the ground. That pain, that is what took me back to the darkness far more than any stitches could.

And then I heard her voice.

"El... El, please. Come back to me. Open your eyes. Don't leave me."

I tried for her; I try to hold on, but my own arrogance nearly killed us all. My own self-importance in thinking I was better than anyone took away one of the beings in my life that I held most dear and then put the other two at risk. They were still at risk even now.

Where was I? We were an easy target.

I tried to move. To get up. I have to get up and protect everyone.

I felt a squeeze on my hand and I turned to see Katherine.

"El, you have to relax. Calm down. Please. It is okay. You are safe. We are safe." I started to shake my head and I felt the fear rise. She is not safe, as long as the book is in her possession, they will keep hunting.

It was like she read my mind.

"El, Daniel sent the book to the publishers. Snippets have already been leaked. It has gone to all the national media. It is okay, no one can hurt me now. If they did everyone would point the finger at James. He would be the only person with a motive."

I felt myself start to relax. She was so smart, so brave. She had kept herself safe, and in the process me and Aveline. Kit... Kit was on me. He was my mistake; I should have trained him better. Made him less protective, something, anything, so he would be here now with me, curled up in a heavy lump on my feet.

I tried to move my toes but I couldn't easily. It was like there was a dead weight laid across my legs and feet. I looked down.

"Kit!" My first word came out as a croak, but he heard it loud and clear and I felt his tail thump against me as I reached down to stroke him. My fingers curled through his thick orange fur then grazed over his freshly shaved patch where I could feel the tender wound and threading of his stiches. He let out a contented soft sigh and continued to lay across my legs like a dead weight.

"It isn't exactly allowed, but apparently, we caused quite a storm with our antics. You are being treated as a minor celebrity, and celebrities are allowed to have their wounded comrade-in-arms with them at all times. That and he howled the town down for hours."

"Aveline?" I croaked.

"She is a tough cookie, that woman. She was so brave and strong. Honestly, El," Katherine settled down on the chair beside me, taking my hand tightly in hers, "I was terrified. I was scared for me, for her, for Kit, but we could hear the gun shots. The cries, the grunts, the screams. I know you told us to stay inside, but I just had to know you were okay. I had the gun, when he was on top of you...I was going to shoot him, but I paused for a minute; I was afraid in case it hurt you or something stupid. Aveline just stepped out and *bang*. You and her...you saved me. I would be dead now. He would have killed us all." Her last few words were eaten up by the soft sob that escaped.

"Shhhh," I soothed, only thankful that we were all here, all safe, and we had lived to tell the tale.

"No, I have to say this...I am sorry. I was so angry because I didn't understand how you could kill a person. How that could be your job. Everything about it told me that you must be evil. That you must be some terrible person because only a terrible person could murder. But I know you, I know that you are not that. You are warm, kind, generous, beautiful and brave, and you don't murder innocent people. You murder bad *bad* people, and whilst I must admit it isn't a career path I would choose nor would I recommend, I understand and I love you. I love you, El. I want to know you, completely, no more lies, no more hiding. Will you tell me everything about your life?"

I took a deep breath and swallowed hard, nodding; saliva stung against my throat. Every movement was an effort. I ached from head to toe and my mind was spinning, but I had never been more sure of anything than when I turned and looked at her. Drinking in her beauty, strength, passion and now... her love.

"I love you too, Katherine Scott-Webb."

# 16

"And tonight on the show, we have an on-air live interview with Katherine Scott-Webb. Katherine, welcome to The Late Night Exclusive, thank you for joining us."

I watch her from the studio edge. I lean against the wall in my normal inconspicuous outfit, bright red trousers and a navy-blue shirt with white stripes, I am embracing my inner British-ness with bold patriotic colors in support of my girlfriend's first exclusive interview since her tell-all book was released a few weeks ago to huge media hype.

She crosses her legs and smooths out

an invisible crease from her modest, classy black dress. "Thank you for having me, Richard."

Richard smiles warmly and leans in for the "I am your friend, you can tell me anything" look, but Daniel and I have warned Katherine—Richard Stokes is a viper in designer suits, and she is not to let her guard down for even one sweet second.

"Author of the fastest selling tell-all book of the year? You are always welcome on my couch, dear." He smiles and the audience twitters. I see the flash of Katherine's feistiness.

"Well, firstly, Richard, let me just correct you there. I am not the author of the fastest selling tell-all book of the year, as you put it, rather the author of my autobiography, which documents amongst other things, the nature of the relationship with my ex-husband, and whilst I am sure this is not what you meant, I would hope to clarify that I am not only welcome on your couch because I was a victim of domestic abuse."

Richard Stokes had a reputation for being a loud mouth. His talk show was one of the most watched shows on the network because he had a way of really getting under people's skin. And I mean really provoking them to react in a way that made for great television.

I wasn't sold on the idea of using Richard Stokes as the mouthpiece to push the narrative of Katherine's book, but Daniel felt strongly that it was important for his mother's position as a CEO to come out as a now strong and independent woman.

Because James Webb had lost everything, and whilst the assassination attempt in France hadn't been tied to him, it also had been reported with a lot of open questions in the dialogue, which pointed the media attention his way.

I didn't think he would take it quietly. Men like that never did, so his response had been, "If I broke this woman so badly, how did she go on to build a multimillion-pound empire?"

I had begged Katherine to let me take him out, but apparently, we didn't live like that anymore and I couldn't make an exception for James Webb. So here we were, on national live television, coming out swinging like the beautifully badass, incredible boss bitch that I know she is.

Richard Stokes offers Katherine a smile that doesn't reach his eyes. "Of course, no one on this production team condones any form of abuse whether that is within a marriage or not. It was interesting that some old CCTV footage has been released from a restaurant where your ex-husband can be seen throwing you down the stairs."

"Well," Katherine smiles as she takes a drink of her water, "I am pleased you were able to collaborate the truth, Richard, but I am not sure what your question is."

"I suppose what I am asking, and the nation is too at this point, is how could you stay? How could you stay with a man who did that to you? And then how could you finally leave and say nothing? I mean, your ex-husband nearly became the Prime Minister of this country. He nearly ran this nation and you were happy to let that happen?"

Katherine takes a long slow breath before looking up at Richard Stokes and then directly to the camera lens. "I didn't leave my husband at the time because I loved him and I stupidly thought he would change, that it would get better. And then when I grew stronger, when I saw that it was always going to be that way, he threatened me. He threatened my home, my job, my life, my son, and so I was scared and afraid and alone. The day I left him I thought I would be dead in a few days. I thought he would kill me, but I left anyway for Daniel. I needed Daniel to see that it wasn't okay. That it was not love. It was an illness. A sickness. A monster inside of his father, but that wasn't the way it had to be. As for being happy to let James become Prime Minster... no, I wasn't happy about that. I was terrified that was going to happen and that is why I started writing my story, the truth, so that people could see James Webb for the man he really is and not the suit and fake smile he hides behind every single day."

I watch the audience go quiet, hanging on her every word. She has captured them; they feel her pain and her strength in her total honesty. In the way she has bared her soul with no apology. Just the facts of why she did what she did, the reason she acted the way she had.

I watch as Daniel makes his way through the back room to stand beside me.

"She is doing a great job," he whispers and I smile at him.

"You prepared her well. Richard Stokes is not holding back; he is going for her."

"It is what he does, but I know my Mum. She has this covered." He smiles and I grin back at him.

"Of that, I have no doubt." And I turn my gaze back to the stage.

"How has this release of your book affected your current life?" Richard asks diplomatically. I can feel him toning down his assault on Katherine.

"Well, I mean, has it been easy? No, it hasn't. I have not only had to relive some of the hardest days of my life but I have then had the nation pick them apart. My ex-husband has attacked me again in his own ways that are no longer physically harmful to me, but they have certainly affected my life. I have had grown men, politicians who are elected to run this country, give their opinions on how I am as a woman, a wife, a mother, a business owner. So yes, it has been hard. But, honestly, Richard, I have so many great things in my life now that I am thankful for. I have my business, which is hard work and tiring and stressful, but I love it. I have my son, who is graduating this year, and he is the single best thing that ever happened to me. I am so proud of him, so in awe of his strength, kindness, and compassion that it makes me want to be a better person. And then, I have my partner, Elena."

I feel the heat rise to my cheeks and I look at Daniel in a panic. He looks back at me and laughs. "Oh, come on, did you really think she wasn't going to mention you? She loves you, like a lot."

Richard's eyes lit up. This was the very first of Katherine speaking publicly about a new partner.

"So, Elena was the bodyguard you employed when you feared for your life?"

"Yes, that's right." Katherine smiled confidently, sexily.

"And, Katherine, when you say partner, do you mean romantic partner? You fell in love with your bodyguard?"

"Absolutely, I did. Elena came into my life like a tornado, a whirlwind of chaos and she showed me that love was real and it existed and is beautiful. Every day she makes my world sparkle, she makes my heart beat faster, she pushes me to be braver, bolder, to run faster, to jump higher, to smile wider, to laugh harder. She saved my life—everyone knows that she was stabbed, and nearly died protecting me. But she saved me in another way too." Her eyes seek me out past the glow of the cameras, looking past the beams that light her up until she finds me.

"You saved me in so many ways, and I love you."

# EPILOGUE
## 5 YEARS LATER

I wake up next to her, the hazy morning light coming through the bedroom window in the chateau.

Katherine looks as beautiful as ever, naked in a tangle of sheets, her long dark eyelashes flicker as her body starts to stir in the sunlight. She is so much more confident in her body these days. I don't think her insecurities will ever totally go away, but I do what I can to make her feel beautiful every day.

There are grey roots beginning to creep through her glossy brown hair, her never ending line of regularly scheduled appointments to make her look perfect has lapsed as her happiness has grown. If anything, she looks more perfect for the imperfections. The things that make Katherine beautiful are so much more than the colour of her hair and whether her eyebrows are newly waxed and her nails are done.

Her nails are still done though, actually. She loves having her nails done. I do them for her. I enjoy the intimacy of it, caring for her fingers and toes. We have a gel nail set in the chateau now and I do them for her. The same pale pink shade that has always been her favourite. She loves cherry blossom. When she was a child they used to have a cherry blossom tree in their garden and on or around her birthday every year, it used to rain pink petals. She has never forgotten it. We planted some cherry blossom trees in the grounds of the chateau and although still small, they are starting to bloom with their pale pink blossom and they are stunning, I can't wait to see them grow bigger and rain their own pink petals in our home.

It has been strange adjusting my lifestyle and quitting my previous line of work. On one level, my identity was so wrapped up in that, that it has been difficult to find another self. I cannot imagine myself doing a normal job of any kind. I recovered fully, physically from what happened with Rabinovich. I have scars- of course I do- they certainly aren't the first scars I've ever had. I'll bear the scars of my previous life choices for the rest of my life. But, I have slipped somehow very easily into life as Katherine's wife.

We married three years ago, just the two of us. We ran away to a beautiful greek island and married on the beach. I had never considered marriage as something I might do, but with Katherine, it felt right. It was something that was important to her. She wanted to leave her ex husband and his name behind so she is now Mrs Katherine Volkova. Volkova was my mother's name and something that still makes me happy to think of her. Daniel also chose to change his name to Daniel Volkov- as an adult, it was entirely his choice, but as he makes his own move into politics to try and make our country a better place, it makes me proud that he wants to be associated with us like that.

Daniel visits the chateau often and he is so close to Katherine. He never questioned our love. He sees the happiness in his mother's eyes and although he knows I am the same woman he met in that cafe, he has never mentioned it or questioned it. He seems grateful to me, for keeping his mother safe and for loving her in a way she has waited her whole life to be loved.

Katherine now employs someone to run her business and she spends her time writing. Her autobiography garnered so much attention both for the content, but also for the way that Katherine writes that draws you right into what she is writing and makes you feel everything with her.

She has published three fiction novels since which have both done well and she is now working on a tell-all biography for a famous actress who has spent her career hiding things.

I wasn't sure what I wanted to do next with my life. There are so many options, I don't need money. I made so much money in my career and invested it well, it isn't something I worry about.

When we had settled in ourselves properly to our new lives, I had a thought and I put it to Katherine.

"I think I want to help kids. Not like babies or anything, but older kids, who have had troubled lives, who need help."

We have such a huge home, it seemed like we could open it up to others who might need us.

As much as I hate people, there is a purity to children, like I feel like I might be able to help.

Of course, Katherine was on board, right away. She took to it as though it was her own idea. I think she might have had a big family years ago if her marriage hadn't been so troubled.

Our first foster child was a twelve year old girl called Adele. She was cautious and anxious. We knew bits about her background, but I was sure we didn't know the half of it. We took her temporarily to start with as emergency foster care and eventually we applied to adopt her.

Adele is sixteen now. There have been

difficult times, for sure. She was skinny and withdrawn, poorly educated, difficult in school, but now she is finishing high school with good grades and some close friends. She loves playing in the gyms with me. She wants to study nutrition and strength and conditioning and to maybe work in sport when she is older. I smile when I see her running around my outdoor gym and assault course on the estate with her friends and with Kit. He is older now, but fully recovered from his wound. Luckily no major damage was done. I bloody love that dog.

We have two more kids on foster at the moment with us. They are twins- eight years old- Celeste and Francois, they both have this bright blonde hair just like me and if we are out together people immediately assume I'm their biological mum. We have applied for adoption for them too and time will tell what happens with that.

Katherine wakes up and she is lazy with sleep and she kisses me and nuzzles into me. We both have morning breath but it doesn't seem to matter in the slightest. It is a minute before I realise that Katherine's lazy morning kisses are moving down my body, my neck, my collarbone, my nipples. Katherine has my nipple in her mouth and she suckles it gently, then more insistently and my body comes alive beneath her.

Her mouth is on my stomach, down over a less firm stomach- my training regime is less arduous these days. Her mouth is on my sharp hipbone, her tongue running downwards.

Over the time we have been together, more and more often, Katherine wants me in more and more ways. She is braver, more confident and more inventive. It has been like watching her actually gradually become free before my very eyes, a beautiful butterfly emerging from a chrysalis.

Her mouth is on me now, warm and wet, enveloping my clitoris and suckling in the same way she was on my nipple.

My body is truly alive and awoken now as she begins to lick up and down and brings her fingers to join her mouth. Her fingers push into me and I feel myself moaning loudly.

My want for her still is overwhelming

and all encompassing. Her fingers push harder as she works for my orgasm, she knows she will get her reward. I feel her deep inside me and I feel closer to her than I ever have to anyone.

Sometimes, these days, we tease and edge each other. Sometimes these days we use toys and we have sex in wild places. (less so with kids in the house.)

But, today, it is none of that, she is insistent with her movements and I look down at the flickering dark eyelashes on her closed eyes, the concentration on her face as her mouth works for my pleasure and her messy dark bed hair and I'm overwhelmed with love, lust and everything in between. My body tenses and my back arches and heat rushes through me. I come hard for her mouth and fingers.

She moves up my body and she's smiling and still lazy and bed heady in the early morning light and my sex glistens clear all around my mouth.

She leans in to kiss me and I taste myself on her lips.

"Morning, beautiful," she murmurs.

I have to almost pinch myself.

Everyone thinks it was me that saved her.

Nobody knows, and perhaps not even she does, that in reality, it was her who saved me.

# AFTERWORD

Thank you so much for reading Her Assassin.

There is a film I first watched many years ago when I was a teenager called Point of no Return with Bridget Fonda which is about a female assassin. It was in watching this movie which had violence but also sadness, pain, love and loss and shows the main character desperately seeking something, that began my curiosity into female assassins.

I knew I wanted to create a great female assassin character in one of my books, so I hope Elena lived up on paper to the Elena I had in my head when I wrote her.

## MAILING LIST

On a beach in France, Summer crashes into Max's life and changes everything. This is a hot and heady summer romance. https://BookHip.com/MFPGZAX

## ALSO BY MARGAUX FOX

She was supposed to be catching a criminal, not falling in love with one. getbook.at/Lilysworld

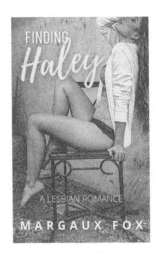

Haley was supposed to be finding herself, can
she do that in the bed of someone else?
getbook.at/Haley

Taylor's new job ideally doesn't involve falling in
love with her beautiful boss. getbook.at/HLI

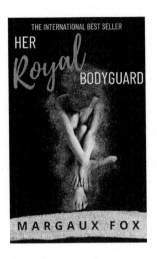

THE INTERNATIONAL BEST SELLER

HER *Royal* BODYGUARD

MARGAUX FOX

Erin is the Princess's Bodyguard. The last thing
that is supposed to happen is that she falls in
love with her.

Printed in Great Britain
by Amazon